One Twin

One Twin

BOOK ONE

Tikat

BOOK COVER & ARTWORK BY ELAINE YOUNG VACHON
EDITING BY ELAINE YOUNG VACHON

Order this book online at www.trafford.com
or email orders@trafford.com

Most Trafford titles are also available at major online book retailers.

Printed in the United States of America.

ISBN: 978-1-4669-0628-0 (sc)
ISBN: 978-1-4269-7674-2 (e)

Library of Congress Control Number: 2011944238

Trafford rev. 01/03/2013

 www.trafford.com

North America & international
toll-free: 1 888 232 4444 (USA & Canada)
phone: 250 383 6864 ♦ fax: 812 355 4082

Contents

This book is dedicated to my Dad, who has taken the last trip home before me. You are to me much missed, never forgotten, still an inspiration. The one who encouraged me to be whom and what I am, without sexist restrictions, always happy to see me break some of those rules. Love ya. See ya on the other side Dad.

Put Put, Tikat over and out . . .

Chapter 1

THE SHARING

JOANNA MILLER GRABBED a stir straw for her hot chocolate at the Flying J Plaza, truck stop in Vaudreuil Quebec. Her waist length hair hung in a single thick jet black braid Blazing blue eyes danced merrily as she stared back at yet another admirer. Caught in the act, he spilt his coffee while trying to nonchalantly look away. With a smile upon her full lips her attention swung towards the sweets offered. Taking stock of what was there, she chose the usual, a honey donut. Her and Sara's favorite.

SARA! Sara. Blinding pain brought her to her knees, causing her to in turn slosh her drink to the floor. A ringing sang in her ears, droning to a deep hum. A splintering pain shattered the back of her head. An explosion of stars swam before her eyes. Ghostly kicks to her ribs wracked her body causing her to jerk in spasms of tortured agony. Now confused, and in shock, her brain seemed to no longer register the truck stop; though physically she was there. Her mind and body hung in a space and time of blind nothingness except for these hellish sensations. A silent scream welled within her to finish in an echoing moan which bounced within Joanna's skull.

"Bitch," growled a far off man's voice as a phantom clout to the jaw caused Joanna to reel to her left.

"You cheep bitch," continued the cruel high pitched voice in a fever of angered hate. "I just asked for a hundred thousand dollar loan, not your f"king life! But now I'm going to take both!" promised the harsh raging male speaker.

An unearthly punch to the stomach doubled Joanna in two completely winding her, "Think you can stop me, stop my dreams little Sara," taunted the man.

"No I tell ya, no, I'm going to have my California health club plus my freedom too!" he screeched before beginning a madman's giggle.

Another ghostly punch to the side of the head reeled Joanna to the right, "Feeling sore Sara," cooed the voice, "Oh! You're unconscious poor darling." he jeered, "or playing dead!"

Joanna felt her self being lifted by strong arms. Soon replacing those arms was a hard cold railing upon her bare back. "Well, well, my darling, let's try some water to help you answer my needs?" the man said giving her an eerie slobbering kiss upon the brow. Then came a mighty final shove from those ghastly murdering hands.

"Drown my beautiful wife, drown, all I need is your cash!" he stated as a matter of fact.

"Goodbye you cheap bitch, you now pay the price of refusing your husband his wish."

Cold air whipped by her, cooling her exposed skin as she turned head over heels. Dizzy, along with that scary falling sensation, she knew she rushed towards the hard impact of the waiting water. An instant later she felt the horrible enforced opening of those frigid waters as it swallowed her whole and uncaring. She felt the heavy wet clothing of November dragging her down to the bowels of the lake.

"JOANNA," came the heart wrenching last thought of Sara, her identical twin. Then nothing. In that chamber of horrors within her mind's eye, was a total silence, emptiness, worse than the shattering events of before. The deep absence of light, sound, air and life itself!

Total numbness. A deep sensation of being utterly alone washed in over her.

The sharing now finished, left her with the horrible truth that swamped her with the engulfing comprehension of being now but "one twin."

Chapter 2

DECISION

As if a switch had been thrown, Joanna became conscience of the reality surrounding her. She was stretched out on the Flying J's concrete floor, hair unbound from the fury of her ordeal. Presently wild compared to the once discreet braid, it now flowed around her like the black waters of Sara's grave. Worried voices of the cashier, security guard and bystanders came to her in catches. At first fuzzy, far-off, then they became as a C.B. zeroing in with static than clearing.

"Mam, are you all right, are you ill, do you need a doctor?" asked a worried cashier in English.

"Madame, ça va, est-vous malade, en avez vous besoin d'un médecin?" inquired the concerned security guard in French, asking her if all was well as well as if she needed a doctor.

They both helped a dazed Joanna to her feet. She struggled emotionally and physically to get there plus hold a grip on reality. The sharing phenomenon burned brightly in her mind. Her body was stunned from the confusing messages that her brain had sent it. Joanna gulped air, heaving in two or three breaths, confirming to herself that she wasalive and could breathe. She shook her head, causing her long mane to ripple. Many onlookers admired her for her simple beauty, even in this unconventional state.

"I'm O.K, thanks, please don't worry, I'm fine," She answered trying to soothe the cashier. "Ça va, merci, ne t'inquiet pas S.V.P, je suis bien," Joanna, being bilingual, answered in French saying to the guard, not to worry she was well. He in turn, asserted her declaration with a stern nod, thus proceeded to shoo away the curious onlookers.

Squaring her shoulders, Joanna pulled herself up tall to her full five foot five inches. Though not impressive in stature she was imposing in presence, personality as well as vitality. The fresh horror of her sisters' death haunted her. She stood plagued; confused by the whole vivid violent experience. After a moment the phantom pains began to fade in strength. Hopefully convincing them of her statement of well being, she held in check her despair and unushered tears. This seemed to console some straggling inquisitive onlookers, as well as the worried yet smiling cashier who returned to her station.

The guard then turned towards Joanna, asking her to join him in his coffee break, jokingly saying, "have one on me little lady." Joanna understanding the tactful undercurrents agreed as she was escorted to a comfortable and quiet cabin table of the adjoining "Country Buffet" restaurant.

Half an hour later, she had downed a cup of coffee in addition to chatted aimlessly with the guard named Serge. That is discussing randomly everything except for what was on her mind. Having deemed enough time had elapsed, she stood to take leave. Barely managing to thank him in her hurry, she excused herself. As she left she threw over her over her shoulder, "thank you," confirming that a few hours of sleep was the needed remedy to all her evils. She turned the corner and left. Heading straight for the door, Joanna hoped to not get tied up by friends or goodwill wishers as she absently waved to a besotted worried Serge.

Wishing her hastily retreating back a goodnight, satisfied that she was physically well, Serge had reseated. For a moment he wondered who the real, strong willed, yet troubled young woman was? Signing to the waitress to put it on his bill, he stood leaving to reassume his duties. All that evening, Joanna, unknowingly was an unsolved mystery to him.

Hoping to avoid a lady who seemed to seek her out she hastily ducked behind the rack of stuffed toys. Joanna then be-lined it to the last row. She chose to cross the store width by the refrigerated section, coming out by the game room. Not complying with her habitual visit to the TV. Lounge by the laundry and showers. She aimed for the side door which loomed at last in front of her.

J.J gave an answering wave, accompanied by a half hearted smile to an old acquaintance's inquiry as to how she was; she then made her escape. Getting closer to that door she came face to face with another road buddy. Having answered his questions she begged out of the conversation saying she was bushed, heading once more for that door.

This time she made it without being interrupted.

Pushing open that blessed door, she appreciated the gust of cold which seemed to put out some of the fire in her warm cheeks. Luckily for a change her black cherry, 97 Peterbilt was parked in the front row a short distance away. Standing proud her home on wheels all 20,100 pounds of tractor van seemed to beckon to her. It offered the much needed seclusion and protection, akin to a steel set of mother's arms waiting to embrace the flustered child. It stood in wait with its gleaming Texas bumper, and 8 inch hockey stacks in the waning light of the setting sun. The two stainless steel 150 gallon tanks, along with the step trunks were buffed, by hand well rubbed to a steady shine. The aluminum wheels luster caught the eyes of many a trucker, along with the American flag radiator blanket. The polished aluminum windshield sun-visor served well just as it added to the looks, plus of course no doubt about it the eagle hood ornament with its spread wings spoke of strength, freedom, and the will to do what must be done to survive. All this gave her truck the eye arresting, "American style" look.

The Peterbilt was pinned to a fifty-three foot utility reefer, full of Detroit diesel motors of the series 60 model, two V8's and one V12 for the airport snow-plow. Joanna, ahead of her schedule on the return trip from Michigan was to deliver this load the next day. Half a day and night was supposed to be freely disposed for a shower, a hair wash, maybe even doing her nails, supper and a leisurely chew the rag with other truckers. But now, all Joanna wanted was the welcoming privacy of her Peterbilt. It continued to beckon to her, purring with its finely tuned Cummins 14n+ motor, humming at its fixed idle throttle of one thousand RPM's.

Let's just say today hadn't turned out at all like the day to relax she had planned. No, it had to be the worst waking nightmare she could have ever imagined. Hastily unlocking the door of the cab with shaking hands she at last attained the security of solitude. Climbing aboard into the velvet and leather interior, she kicked off her steel capped work boots.

Grief stricken and free to be her self, within the intimacy of the darkening warm interior she laid her head upon the steering wheel. Sinking down into the black velvet seat, her shoulders slumped with the expiring of an almighty sigh. The false facade of bravo fell. The sigh turned to a moan, as tears brimmed over into a waterfall of once suppressed emotions. Crying herself dry, she felt wasted, small, so very alone even though a set of loving watchful eyes kept a tag on her.

Exhausted, both emotionally and physically, she raised herself from her seat. Dragging herself to her bunk, she closed off the section to undress. She slipped into a fretful tormented sleep, filled of dreams of days and gone by.

In one of her dreams, the now twenty five year old was a family again. She was sitting in the kitchen of the family home, having a Sunday breakfast surrounded by all her now dead loved ones. Mom and Sarah were there. Mom also known as Sadie to all her friends, smiled while giving as good as she got from her teasing husband. Dad, Joey Miller known to all of Frampton, and the surrounding areas, was once again alive here too, full of vigor. He beamed mischievously yet proudly at his girls. Though the roof had snow on it as his identical twin daughters loved to tell him, his strength both physically, and of character were felt, respected in addition to loving him.

The chimneys of the steam-engine run sawmill billowed gray smoke from it. The old flat nose truck hummed than hawed outside waiting for its driver to go get logs for making into ties for the railroad. It was the year 95; Sara was not yet married to Brian Thorp.

That blond, blue-eyed, good looking, muscle bound egotistical, money grubbing, murdering son of a bitch! In that dream . . . they still laughed together, ate and were a family.

Joanna, first born of the identical twins was named after her Dad, known as Joe. So Joe was feminized to Joanna. Sara, born 15 minutes after on that day of October 26th was named after her Mom without the "h" on the written name. The dotting parents felt that this way the twins had a bit of each of them. In order to tie the girls together as twins, both names were finished with an "a". Time tested, it proved a good choice of names. Joanna was the tomboy of the two and Sara the lady, like her mother.

The time zone of her happy illusions that existed only in memories now changed. Joanna was twelve again. She had just fallen through the roof of old McMillan's abandoned wood rotted barn. She lay twisted upon the hood of the truck she was trying to investigate.

The truck everyone seemed to of forgotten about except her. She had hoped to secretly get it going again, paint it up and surprise everyone.

They, the grateful adults in her childish cherished fantasy would then give the truck to her; Joanna, the proud rescuer of this solid yet rotting hunk of scrap. Yet once again things hadn't turned out as they were supposed to. For there she was, a few miles from home in an abandoned barn, far out in a field of an old farm which no one ever visited anymore. Joanna, having told no one of her secret wish or plan, to boot hurt like hell. On top of it, she was winded and even if she could scream no one would hear her. But to her surprise after thirty minutes of agony she heard the worried voices of her parents along with Sara.

It turned out she had a broken leg, a fractured left wrist, plus badly bruised ribs. Therefore apart from getting an enormous ear full from her parents, having casts, being grounded for a month, not seeing her wishful vision come true; she was not able to go on the school outing. To top it off, she only got three days off from school. But the worst of it all was Joanna, is right handed; therefore she still could write her school work. No it wasn't at all according to plan, nor were there many advantages.

That had been the first time Joanna and Sara had mind shared. Sara had vividly experienced the heart stopping fall, as well as shared the wrenching pain of her sister's landing. Joanna's fearful thinking and pain had become Sara's for those few moments. Therefore the twin receiver was able to pinpoint Joanna's whereabouts as well as situation. Sara had gotten her parents hurriedly together leading them directly to her grateful sister.

The twin's parents had thought Sara had been in on the trump. Therefore they grounded her for a month also. This of course did far from please Sara, who also missed out on the school outing. She however didn't get three days off from school, or the special attention lavished on Joanna the part invalid from their dotting parents.

Peeved, Sara had gotten even by letting Joanna's pet snake loose outdoors. Sara, who had an aversion to begin with to all snakes and especially this one, had claimed it had been an accident when she had tried to feed it for Joanna. This story was believed by all except the owner of the beloved reptile. To tell the truth, the only one saddened by this event was of course Joanna. Their Mother shared Sara's aversion to snakes, and their father after having found Slithers in his sock drawer one time hadn't exactly loved him either. But they did make up soon afterwards, furthermore were as always close, sharing their secret of mind sharing as a special bond between them. Of course, Joanna, who knew Sara was innocent of being in lead with her, believed Sara's claim. How else could she of had known so much; the when, where and how without being there? After all, weren't they even, Slithers was gone plus Joanna was unable to participate in many family things, leaving Sara, to get most of the attention on those occasions.

Once again the time zone of her walk through memory lane changed, and Joanna was on her way to Virginia to deliver a load of paper for Quebecor. She relived the devastating feeling of fear. That horrible impression that a piece of her heart had been wrenched from her! Totally causing it to come to an abrupt stop, and ceasing to exist. So overwhelmed by the sensation of loss, Joanna had been obliged her to pull her truck up onto the shoulder of the highway.

Sitting there eyes brimming over she had shared with Sara the visit of the Montreal police who had came to announce the death of their beloved parents. She felt the apprehension in addition to the stark panic of Sara upon seeing the two officers on the cottage doorstep.

Felt the stiffening of Sara's muscles as she forced herself to walk like a mechanical doll to answer the summons of the doorbell. She could see and feel Sara's shaking hand take hold of the doorknob as she eyed the police through the door window. Joanna struggled with Sara fighting the tight knot in her throat before she was able to speak.

The officers, respectful in their uniforms were uncomfortable with the bad tidings they had in the line of duty to tell. At odds they shifted weight from one foot to the other. At first they did not seek eye contact. In their dilemma they cleared their throats, began to verify if they were at the right cottage, reading the address from their Father's worn brown leather wallet. The other officer held behind his back their Mother's blackened battered straw purse for identification. Joanna reluctantly lived this as Sara lived the moment.

Together their hearts sank when the officer asked if Sara recognized the purse and wallet. Joanna experienced the helplessness as Sara's legs turned to jelly. She shared the dizziness as well as heard the far-off roar resembling an ocean wave that came sweeping Sara into unconscious bliss for a mere few minutes. She lived with Sara the confusion of coming to upon the sofa of the cottages' front room. The twins shared the recollection of the grizzly past quarter of an hour along with the shock of the dawning truth. Joanna, and Sara, were orphans, stripped of their most precious earthly cornerstone, their anchor to what was their world. Both their parents had perished, hopefully before their vehicle burst into flames.

The horror of this thought made the reality doubly tormenting. The not knowing if they suffered the burning of the vicious hot flames as their lives ebbed from them. It hit, the unjustness, the senselessness of the untimely and ghastly death of two loyal, good, loving, harmless people.

Two parents who sought only to live their lives happily together, caring for each other and their daughters, hoping one day to be grandparents.

They didn't deserve to die, had so much to live and hope for. Why did this happen to them, how could this now be the end of their story? How, when many chapters could yet and should of been written into their shortened life saga? No, that too hadn't turned out as it could have been. The emptiness of the loss of the twin's parents stayed with them as well as the unanswered questions which faded yet always present in the shadows of their thoughts.

Brian of course, as usual when needed wasn't to be found. He was off on a business trip to California. He sought the approbation of his distant unknown Uncle for a future Health Club upon the said Uncle's many acres of land. The sheet of paper supposedly left in case of emergencies beside the telephone with the address and number to join him . . . had vanished. It had been thought to of been thrown out by the cleaning lady.

Brian, phoned only after the burial, claiming once told of the tragedy, that Sara should have called him. Which of course due to the circumstances had been impossible? He showed up a week after, saying however sorry he was . . . that to of had cut short his business trip wouldn't of changed anything. After all he couldn't bring them back, and the burial had already taken place. He however of course assisted Sara and Joanna at the reading of the will. Brian, being the perfect hypocrite, oozing with concern for the twin sisters, acted the loving gallant husband to Sara.

The will of course, divided the considerable hard-earned wealth of the parents equally between the girls. The sisters equally divided the responsibilities between themselves to continue the sawmill product ability and the caring for the family home, and lands. A well known worker, and assistant to Joey Miller was put in charge of the overseeing of the mills functions. He also became live in caretaker along with his wife of the family home and lands. Clara Catherine and George Tisson always received the twins in their family home with smiles and home cooking. This had eased the pain of the girls, plus filled a void in the Tisson's lives, for they had had the misfortune of being childless.

Sara, an accountant took control of all that pertained to that department. Joanna managed the mechanical needs and production of the mill, making the final decisions concerning the lands as well. The Tisson's ran the mill daily. The elderly couple preserved the twin's material homage and memories of their parents. The family home continued conserving their carefree, fun filled active childhood souvenirs of days past. The arrangement worked well answering the needs of all concerned. The twins had agreed upon this arrangement as they agreed upon most everything. That is of course, everything except Sara's choice of a husband, which had caused a bit of a rift. But the twins love for each other had even overcome this.

Sara and Joanna, though well bestowed upon by their inheritance, were already both very well established in their own right. So the money to them in a sense held no real importance. However after what had happened today, Joanna now knew that to Sara's conniving husband it was an all important fact. Brian's dream of yet another Health Club made him consider the twins bad luck as a blessing. To the girls, their true inheritance was rather an aching loss accompanied by an empty void, resulting from the death of their parents. The only one the money seemed to preoccupy, Joanna was certain of, was that gold digger, Brian!

"Sara, oh Sara, why did you fall in love with that bastard who sent you to your watery grave?" And with the cry of her own voice she woke up to a painful reality.

Stiff and haunted by the illusive shadows of bygone days, she, Joanna, felt full of grief and anger. She was not only humanly alone in the privacy of her truck, but in life itself. J.J sat there numb, as the dawning of this truth took root. It was now up to her. The rekindled burning of the mind sharing like coals fanned into flames, branding into her being the fact that she was the only survivor of her immediate family. That is apart from Brian, who knew what had just happened. The need of the present moment was now to decide what to do!

The tear stained, yet alluring face hardened as she thought of her choices. She could either go to the police to be taken for a harebrained sicko looking for unproved trouble, or get even with the sawed off hunk of cow plop.

Getting even appealed to her sense of rightness, much more than passing for a moronic broad. Getting him back for taking what was dearest to her, quickened her sluggish blood flow as her heart began to pound in a war dance rhythm. The excitement of getting what was dearest to him would be the only thing to quench the vengeful thirst overtaking her. These consuming ideas grew putting her into the hunter's frame of mind. She began to plan how to stock and lure her pray. The glee of getting Brian where it would hurt him the most gave her the strength to continue. The now dreary forecast of her life without Sara took on a different light. The wrath of this twin was held in check like a leashed animal by the promise of getting its due. When the time came she would take pleasure in seeing him squirm. Way into the wee hours of the new day she planned how to go about it. The anger within slowly calmed as she put her emotions on the back seat to make way for the cool calculations of her revenge.

She made a silent vow, an oath to her line. Brian Thorp wouldn't profit by the death of Sara. The Miller's money would not be used to fulfill the fancies of this murderer. He would rue the day he killed, and lived with this knowledge in fear like the animal he was. Hunted and haunted by one twin.

"You live on in me Sara!" Joanna said out loud as if speaking to the spirit of her twin as she verbally confirmed it to herself. She went on to firmly voice her vow again, sealing the oath to all the Miller's lineage.

Chapter 3

STEP INTO
SARA'S SHOES

THE INSISTENT BUZZING of an alarm clock at last made its way through the crowded thoughts of its owner. Joanna groaned as she rolled over to stare at its luminous face in the sleeper's curtained gloom. The clock's flat face stated 6:00 am as it persistently buzzed back at her. Joanna swatted the thing, slapping it into silence. Then rolled over onto her back like a pouting child, cheeks puffed and lips puckered shut. The night had not improved her humor or thoughts towards Brian.

Solomon, who had been watching wanted to join in the fun of the clock attack at first, however he quickly sensed mistress was not playing this morning. Therefore he backed down with reptilian grace or was it survival instinct?

Never having had been much of a morning person; Joanna's habit was for the first ten, fifteen minutes of the dawning of a new day to lay on her back. Stretched out like a cat she relished the comfort of her bunk. Solomon, her three and one half foot pet iguana crawled onto her tummy. He was waiting for a sign from her granting permission to adventure closer. He knew his mistress well.

"Ok, come on and get your hug old boy, mom's got a lot to do today," she said stretching to rub the flat head. "Just me and you now!" she stated as a sad truth.

Solomon joyfully scrambled to rub cheeks and his forked tongue slithered a kiss tasting the salty tears on the skin of his mistress. He \ continued his direction up to the crown of her head. There he blissfully cuddled up in the flowing mane spilled over the pillow. He enjoyed the perfumed odor along with the silky feeling of Joanna's hair. Resting with one forearm near her forehead, he took a comical pose of the thinker. He waited, wallowing in this comfort. Sol knew usually Joanna would soon get up causing him to loose his choice position.

Mistress seemed even more preoccupied this morning, but his limited brain for the moment did not allow him to grasp the why. He felt stress in her taught muscles, and the atmosphere of the sleeper held something new he couldn't define. One thing he did decide was he didn't much like this feeling. His reptilian wisdom told him not to play his customary games this morning. That meant not to nip her ears playfully, nor demand to be fed or walked before mistress was ready too. No waiting was good, and that's what he did.

A hollow feeling had settled within Joanna. A sort of an aftershock which made her and Solomon resemble each other. Both in a way were cold blooded as they began this chapter of their lives. She too lay motionless as the gentle vibrations of the well tuned motor hummed its mechanical lullaby, gently rocked by November's gusts of wind. Warm air washed over her body from the vents, though they did nothing to diminish the cold empty feeling within.

Reptile and human were both frozen in thought as well as time for this instant. Silently they accompanied each other, waiting for one or the other to move. Joanna, usually after her lay about was ecclesiastic, jumping out of bed to greet the challenge of the day; after saying a little prayer for loved ones and protection for all on and off the road. Today she was not impulsive.

A deadly calm had enveloped her. Today she was a woman with a mission other than doing her job while accomplishing the many tasks it entailed.

Flexing her muscles, a fair warning to Solomon who scooted out of the way, she sat up. Looking with disdain at the time, an hour had passed. After a visit to the portable loo, she quickly dressed, made the bunk then fed Solomon. J.J. made due with a hasty makeshift breakfast of a cinnamon bun along with an orange she'd found in the refrigerator. A swig of juice washed it all down. Having done the recap of her log book, she grabbed Solomon's leash and coat.

The well trained reptile climbed onto her knee to be dressed. He loved his walks. But Sol felt by the draft of the open window that they were no longer south. Though nature called, he didn't relish the icy cold. He did however enjoy the attention he got as Joanna did her round of inspection, both from mistress along with spectators alike.

Climbing back into the truck after heaving Solomon up first, Joanna's trained eyes strayed to see if all was in place ready for travel. Verifying the numerous gages in the dash she decided against the need to fuel for the two tanks were at the half mark. She finished filling in her logbook, checked in her mirrors then made ready to leave the parking area.

Solomon, undressed took his kingly position upon the headrest of the passenger seat, digging in his claws in preparation for the shifting of the gears at take off. The setting out was usually smooth, but to his choice position, it was something to watch out for. He knew from experience, having at the beginning landed not so gracefully on the dash; getting an undesired look at the hood; all the one hundred seventeen inches of the Pete's nose.

The eighteen wheels began to crunch the ice as they turned. They were on their way to deliver their load; heading to a new set of beginnings in which the two would travel new roads in life as well as upon the map. Their destination nor estimated time of arrival were not pinpointed on a dispatchers plan nor known ahead. It was to be written day by day from their hearts, wits, and circumstances presented to fit in with what J.J. planned. All that was to be crammed in with everyday life along with work. She pulled out of the exit entering the highway.

A rough, jovial, masculine voice boomed from the C.B, having spotted her entrance. His voice shattered the quiet thoughts of the Pete's occupants, "J.J. where ya heading, going my way doll?"

"Hi to you too Bad-Boy, don't think so, going to drop my load and than visit Sara to see if she wants to come for the next ride." Joanna answered with a smile in her voice that was not on her face.

"Dang once I've dropped, I have a pickup near by, than to Boston I go," lamented Bad-Boy, "sure you lovely ladies won't be going my way?"

"Nope, not this time, maybe the next," at this moment Joanna's laugh was real as the smile she wore, "We'll still beat you on the black ribbon any time, your old Mac has trouble keeping up with us on the hills," she jibed as she clasped her eighteen double overdrive floor bound shift stick lovingly.

"Ah don't be mean to the bulldog, still got that lizard, Solomon?" he asked, as the lizard in question hearing his name looked questioningly at Joanna. He winked as if he knew what was going on.

"Yep want to borrow him?"

"Hell no, keep him away from me, he bit me last time I patted you on the back!"

"He was just letting you know you'd crossed territories that's all."

"Ya, well say hello to Sara for me, my second favorite lady after you and my wife o.k., ten four turning off here."

"Will do, have a good one Bad-Boy, putt, putt." Joanna said. Step one had just been put into motion of the hunt.

Traffic was as always heavy in this district. Chockfull of impatient four wheelers trying to get ahead, be it over or under the truck. They didn't seem to care or realize the difficulties they caused big rigs or their drivers; such as their cutting off or in at short notice. Joanna grimaced as she swerved to go around one of them doing a showmanship of downshifting, and than up shifting again. Maybe due to the size they thought trucks were loving parents? Maybe even well trained "Big Dogs," who unconditionally wouldn't do them any harm; rather than the heavy machinery they were. Being big the rigs demanded both space to roll as well as to stop. Yet like some greedy adolescents, certain drivers dangerously hogged the road or claimed their territory rudely. Of course, some truckers too could be aggressive on the road. Joanna however was a precautious driver; they who weren't so unless for a certain reason irked her.

Her load was delivered, the dispatch called and the trailer swept out in readiness for the next load. Joanna now pulled into the parking of a shopping center. J.J felt her rig would be less of an obstacle parked on the outskirts of the shopping center's parking space; well out of the way for the others. She shut everything down.

Solomon warm and lazy in the sun just lifted his head questioningly, then went back to sleep. He understood He could not always follow her.

Joanna went into the sleeper to shrug out of her work clothes. Pulling on a turtleneck instead of her usual under shirt and covering flannel shirt. Slipping on a woolen ankle length skirt instead of the every day jeans she was transformed into a becoming feminine woman. From the compartment under the bed she took out a pair of women's high heeled boots to replace her steel capped work ones. The dramatic change made her even more eye-catching. Little did she know how often she haunted many lusty males' dreams.

As J.J. brushed her strong, healthy, waist length hair she dreaded the next hour to come. Sara and Joanna were identical twins, but Sara preferred her hair a little over the shoulder to enable easy styling and fussing. Joanna preferred the quick fix of braids or ponytails. To tell the truth . . . to Joanna, her long hair was her mark of distinction between the twins from afar. Now it could be so in reality no longer. With firmness she scooped up her wallet, making sure Solomon was presently comfortable. She then with determination headed to the mall's hairdresser's appointment she'd made via cell phone.

Now for the second time the horrified hairdresser looked at Joanna straight in the eyes through the mirror, "You are sure now aren't you?"

Joanna gulped, replying again with a wavering voice in return, "braid it it then cut the hank off at the length I told you please, I want to keep it as a souvenir."

The hairdresser did as she was asked, regretting almost as much as her client the action. The woman bound the hair for future use as a hair piece. It could be added on in certain hairstyles with a clip for fastening. Joanna's thick luscious braid outshone the many hairpieces for sale at the counter.

Her work done the hairdresser proudly presented her artistry to her client for inspection. Joanna inspected it well pleased. She now smiled as she thanked her in return for her troubles. Taking out her wallet J.J. paid her bill leaving a handsome tip.

Once again glancing into the salon's mirror she was struck by the fact it felt as if Sara was staring back at her. However, laying her traps was her major preoccupation at this moment, so it was good thing. This task accomplished, it was go to the next part of the plot; which was to in reality step into Sara's shoes.

Back in the cab of her truck she called for a taxi. Using the number she had found posted on the mall wall by the pay phone. She made arrangements for him to pick her up in ten minutes at the center door. For this step she was a bit nervous, but knew it would be the key to Brian's undoing. It would bring doubts to his success as a murderer.

Step three was in motion.

Plugging in the full length heating mattress pad, she pulled down the blankets, installing a confused Solomon. He wondered where all mistresses' hair went? She locked up, leaving to meet the cab driver.

Once in the back seat of the cab J.J. gave instructions to go to Sara's all season cottage as if it were her own. She began to chat with the driver telling a tale as to how she had lost her key. The story once told implied she would have to stop first at their part time cleaning lady's, Mme. Cheveau's, to have the door opened for her. She then continued her story saying how her husband, Brian, would still be at the health club. Not wanting to disturb his day's work, well this was the best way to proceed. Also the best way to not let him know that when she'd taken her fall she had lost her key again. Sara had been known to lose keys.

"I still feel stiff you know," she had lamented realistically, pulling in the cabbie by his strings of pity for a lady in distress; marking him if questioned.

The kind concerned cabby offered to take her to see a good doctor he knew first. Joanna refused saying that it would pass, proclaiming that to explain her fall would take way to long as well as embarrass her. Finally they pulled up in front of Mme. Cheveau's.

The woman came out to see who it was. Seeing Joanna she exclaimed, "Ah! Mme Thorp I have already done the cleaning today."

"Good," replied Joanna smiling at her luck and success, "but I took a nasty spill yesterday and lost my key, could you be so kind as to open the door for me, I shall get a few things and be on my way for two to four weeks."

"Of course, you are well I hope. Going on a trip again are we, for work or with your sister?" The curious woman asked.

"Yes another trip, please hurry the cabby is waiting," she answered waylaying the woman without letting out too much.

"My yes, sorry, right away," replied the immediately flustered woman, "I myself must get over to do Mme. Demoine's cleaning. I'll open up then you can lock up afterwards before leaving. I'm sure you have a spare key?" exclaimed the woman as she crossed over into the Thorp's yard.

"That will be fine," Joanna answered as she turned to ask the cabby to drive around to the Thorp's back door to wait. She then followed the little lady now in full gear. The flustered cleaning lady was already fumbling with the lock.

Once inside she expelled a sigh through puffed cheeks, and to her surprise giggled. Pulling herself up, she quickly inspected the lower floor of the cottage, which was neat, holding no sign of Brian being present.

She rushed upstairs to inspect the upper rooms before returning to the master bedroom.

Pulling out the suitcases from under the bed she proceeded to fill them. She took both things that Sara would for a ride with her, or a business trip. J.J. remembered to also take the jewelry box, along with the vanity case filled with Sara's traveling makeup and vanity kit. She went to the place Sara hid her credit cards in addition to bank books when she wasn't carrying them. A place hid from Brian since Sara had caught him gambling a few times. Next she opened the family safe that was kept there. Joanna took out jewelry, keys to safety deposit boxes, stocks in addition to bonds. Next came family financial documents, along with the papers. Then J.J. took out all the family deeds, wills, loose cash, all that was important, or of a value. Brian not knowing the safes' combination wouldn't let that stop him for long. She smirked, imagining his surprise once he discovered his goodies gone after getting it opened God knows how.

Two big suitcases, one pack sac, one vanity case and a huge brief case stood in a now messy room ready to be taken. Joanna knew that this in itself would make Brian wet his pants, setting the panic button to really worried. Of course these extra's would of had cluttered her truck, but by providence she had a little apartment that she had acquired last week. One that even Sara had not yet known of. She would leave most of it there.

"Oops must get the Halloween doll!" she said to herself.

After hauling the luggage to the back door, she had the driver stow them in the trunk while she rushed to the cellar to get it. It was a life sized doll the twins had made years ago, sporting a black wig and with a mould of their faces for its identity. They jokingly had said they were triplets that Halloween, Sara was the brains, Joanna the get up and go, and the third the dead drunk. Brian probably didn't even know of its existence, or remember it.

Dusty and stinky it hung in the far recess of discarded junk within the damp walls of the cellar. Joanna had bought an army stow away bag to transport this particular object while at the mall. She shoved their look alike into the bag.

Once upstairs again she joyfully smashed the wedding picture on the mantle, locked up, leaving the cottage. From the doorjamb J.J. eyed the not so faraway lake. She held tears in check knowing it was the unmarked grave of her sister. She had the cab driver take her to a hotel that Sara was well known at. She asked the porter to watch her luggage till Joanna came to get them. That done she had the cabdriver take her to the mall, saying she would finish her shopping knowing now what she needed. Paying the cabby she waved him off till he was out of sight, and legged it back to her truck. She was glad that part was over, plus the imagining of Brian's reaction to it all took the edge off the pain that ached within.

Joanna started the truck up, turned on the heaters full. Next she went back into the sleeper to change back into herself. Solomon wasn't on the bed, but after a few panicked moments of searching she found him curled up on her cut braided hair, comfortable and pleased with himself.

"Ok. Boy, you can wear it when I'm not!" she giggled taking her swath of hair to clip into place. Like magic she felt truly herself again. The extra weight of the braid felt good, like a coming home to who she really was.

Step three was complete, onto the next she thought cuddling Solomon, allowing him to ride her shoulder as she settled back into the drivers seat. Both were content as they hit the road again.

Chapter 4

THE DOLL

JOANNA PULLED THE Pete up before her 3 ½ basement apartment. She got out leaving a bewildered Solomon staring at her through the window. She went to her beloved peach condition 1990 ford camper. Started its engine listening to it turn over a bit before she drove it out of the driveway, parking it on the other side of the road. Next she backed the truck still pinned to the trailer into the alley that was allotted her parking space for her rig. Grabbing Solomon, his baby bag of things, along with her pack sac, she went to unlock the porch door. It lead to her down stairs cellar apartment and proceeded in.

While swinging the door wide she exclaimed, "Welcome to our new non mobile home away from home," she said with pride presenting Solomon their new part time living quarters.

Closing the door she let Solomon loose to scout out the small furnished apartment. She had planned on inviting Sara to see the place this week, but thanks to Brian it would never be possible. Tears sparkled in her eyes.

Heaving a sigh she scooped up Solomon again to put him on the bed she had made up before taking her last trip. As she turned up the heat, Solomon spotted the five foot debugged dried leafless birch bark tree in the corner; right away he headed to claim it as his. Joanna smiled at her pet as she turned on the radio to a soft level before closing the door. With his litter box, and the night light on he would be all right there. Hopefully out of most trouble while she went to get the luggage.

Getting Sara's luggage as Joanna proved to be no problem; however, lugging it into the apartment was a little problem. The big problem was the project of washing the big dusty, extremely fowl smelling doll. J.J. took off the head. Next she undid the skin colored plastic face to wash it also. Shampooing the wig, as well as styling it was no fun either. J.J. did all this in the small bathtub.

Drying it at least wasn't so bad, since they had stuffed it with foam. Thank God for foam instead of shavings, or hay or something else equally horrible to clean. The legs and arms were held to the body with Velcro; thank heavens, so they could be detached and dried in the drier individually. She finished her doll care late that evening.

Feeling hungry she had a pizza for herself delivered, plus one chef's salad for Solomon. Better check on the wee lad she thought, and she did.

He wasn't on or under the bed, nor in his tree. Yet she could hear him scratching. It took awhile to think of looking behind the curtains. Drawing them open she began to pull up the blind. Bingo, she found what she had lost. The blind started heaving in all directions. Turned out Solomon was caught up in the material blind by his long nails. Now panicking and in a vile humor his tail whipped side to side.

She cooed to him trying to calm him down. J.J managed to rescue the very indignant and ungrateful iguana. Peeved he thanked her with a whip of his tail. Knowing that it wasn't a mean streak but a nervous reaction to fear, Joanna forgave him grudgingly. It smarted and began to welt on her arm.

"Good job you didn't get my face or I'd of pulled your beard," she said menacingly.

"Should put up a sign, beware of the beast! You're safe now," she said showing him his heating pad in the corner of the room at the foot of his tree.

She knew full well that he would most likely be under the covers with her half way through the night. However, till then she'd show him his new world of living in an apartment.

After feeding her pet, having her lunch, she then bathed to at last go to bed herself. Falling almost immediately once again into a mist of souvenirs along with nightmares.

Unaccustomed to apartment life she was awakened early to the sound of small running feet over her head. Next a loud crash was heard, followed by a wail which startled Solomon. He jumped from under the covers to her pillow. His tongue flicked tasting the air for danger, as his head went from side to side. His tail rose in a curve ready to strike to serve, or protect himself along with his mistress.

Joanna groaned, "Another possessive male!"

She turned to see the time and groaned even louder, "6:30 am!"

This startled the nervous iguana that then began a comical scene of jumping around from one direction to another searching for an enemy. Joanna burst into a giggle thinking now the upstairs people will think they have a nut as a new neighbor.

The morning tension having been broken short by her giggling fit gave her the courage to get up a lot quicker than yesterday. She dressed to begin the routine.

Solomon was still trying to figure out why in this home the windows were so far away from the seats and bed compared to his usual environment. Plus he wondered why there were all those hanging traps to catch him? Having found no explanation he wearily climbed on his mistress's knee to be dressed and leashed for his morning walk. Joanna dressed her pet then headed for the door.

Climbing the steps was fun for Solomon; he began to lower his tail as if to say maybe it isn't so bad. The two looked over the truck and Solomon did his business behind the wheel of the trailer, being a prudish creature when it came to personal affairs.

This done Joanna put him on her shoulder; he climbed to the top of her head to ride her to the corner store for breakfast shopping. Of course some were fascinated, while others horrified with the site. Nevertheless Solomon was pleased with the attention, furthermore J.J was used to these reactions.

Back at the apartment they had their breakfast followed by playtime in the bath for Sol. This was one content as well as spoiled iguana. He even had baby bath toys to nudge around, dodge or swim under, as well as a manmade wooden island to rest on. Yet this reptile loved his m o m m y even more than the good things in his life, Sol taken care of J.J. got to the finer points of the day. Thus Joanna mused as she regarded the doll still in pieces. Half an hour later it was once again in one piece. It sat on a chair, wearing a stuffed bra, and a pair of panties at the table. Joanna added to the doll a pair of stuffed skin colored evening gloves, and then began to do a makeup job on the face. She used Sara's make-up kit for this. Not a makeup artist she went slowly learning as she went. To start with she added fake eyelashes on the eyelids over the glass eyes. Next was painted nails with nail polish on the gloves. She then sat back to admire her work. It was beginning to look pretty good, she thought, adjusting the wig to resemble her own cut hair and Sara's style more.

She took a pair of nylons to strap in the waist giving a more realistic womanly curve to the dolls shape. She adjusted this giving the doll a tummy tuck free of charge. Taking a pair of socks, jeans, along with a

T-shirt she dressed the doll in Sara's clothing, putting on it her favorite jeans coat, and cap topped with her sunglasses to finish the look. Backing up the length of the room her look alike was a masterpiece. Besides, even at 30 miles an hour it should do the job and trick onlookers. Pleased with herself, she sat back to survey her work trying to figure out how she could make it move some.

After pondering the problem awhile, she had a solution which would require metal eye hooks, fish line, safety pins, needle, and thread, in addition to her leather wrist bands she often wore. Luckily she had a few sets.

"Yep, by Joanna I believe it will work!" she exclaimed out loud.

She checked on Solomon who was snoozing in his tree, closed the door as she grabbed her camper's keys. Off she went to the hardware store a few blocks away. She hastily made her purchases then rushed home excited about how so far her plan was coming together. At this moment she hopefully prayed Brian's plans were falling apart.

Out of the camper straight into her truck she went with her stuff. She firstly put a set of metal eyes shoulder width, above the back of the passenger seat. J.J screwed them in tightly to the cabs ceiling. Then she did the same thing over her seat, plus a set in the middle of the ceiling.

This done she went back in to rummage in Sara's jewelry box. Out came two rings Sara often wore. J.J. placed them firstly one upon the middle left finger then the other one on the right pinkie. She secured the rings by tacking them in place with fish line so they wouldn't slip off but serve her planned purpose.

After that she got out her two black studded leather wristbands to work with. Puncturing a small hole in each where the top of her wrist would be she laid them down. Returning to the doll she in driving position; put a strand of fish line through each ring, tied tightly singing the knot. Pulling the strands gave an animatation to the doll like puppet which resembled the lifting of an arm. Joanna pinned the elbow of the right arm to the side of the doll. Now it sort of waved with the right hand and lifted the left arm. Very well, that should work not too bad she thought. The true success would be seen when once on the road.

Solomon began to scratch at the door, so she let him out of the room. He stopped flat in his tracks, blinked, and looked straight at Joanna, than the doll. The race was on straight for the jeans clad leg. Up he went to the shoulder cuddling in tasting what he thought were Sara's cheeks. However, the outcome was getting make-up all over himself as he rubbed against it. The iguana sported lipstick, eye shadow along with skin toned blush and foundation. Believe me, he did not look too good, nor did the Sarah doll either.

"Dang, dang, dang!' exclaimed Joanna pulling off her stunned pet. Grumbling she cleaned him up to once more place him in the bedroom.

The dolls white T-shirt had to be re washed, and this she did. J.J decided tougher measures were needed for the face work. Using crazy glue she glued back on the eyelashes. This pleased her to see how well they stuck without melting. Just adding the slightest film of Vaseline over the skin colored plastic of the face gave it a livelier appearance. The powdered blush now stuck well onto the face instead of the liquid one. Then she returned to the hardware store to buy some water based non luster, quick drying spray varnish. Then she returned to finish the job at home.

Back at her drawing board she painted lipstick back on the doll as well as eye shadow. She cut the extra pair of eyelashes to the shape of eyebrows then glued them on. After brushing them into shape, and taking off the wig along with the clothes again, she sprayed the whole face with the varnish; J.J. rested as she waited the said hour.

Once the doll was dressed again, it was testing time. Solomon was let loose. But Sol turned his back on the doll, as if to say, "This is not a dumb iguana here, won't do it again."

Joanna wise to his weakness put some cheese cut small on the dolls shoulder. This of course was an invitation that he couldn't resist. The face held but the cap and hair went awry; so the wig got tacked on with fish line. The cap having a sturdy foundation stayed on now allowing the doll to be certified Solomon proofed. It looked all in all, pretty good, as realistic as possible. Joanna now had her Sara doll companion com traveling decoy.

Pleased she almost purred as she thought, "Yes another step done towards driving Brain around the bend. She smirked, enjoying the taste of sweet revenge.

Chapter 5

WITHDRAWING

THE NEXT MORNING Joanna and Solomon were less dramatically awakened. The cell phone by the bed buzzed out in its mosquito buzz. A groping hand felt for it, found it, and dropped it on the floor. Solomon, as usual jumped on it, scratching and whipping it. He hated that irking sound! This thing truly bugged him. Every chance he had he attacked the phone when it spoke out with viciousness. Joanna sitting up watched the show sleepily. It at last stopped ringing.

"Ok. Boy, its dead, can mommy have it now?" Joanna asked the reptile who proud of his conquest stocked victoriously to his litter box to earlier than usual let go.

Knowing full well who it must be, Joanna picked up the phone to check the call in absence. It was her dispatcher. She called him back.

"Rick, Joanna here," pause, "Yep Solomon killed it again," pause, "Sure you knew I'd phone back, hey I woke up, just slow down a bit, in fifteen minutes I'll jump over you ten times chubby," she laughed back.

"Where, to Florida, ya will do," she affirmed, "what is the delivery date?" she asked, "and where to?"

"You and your reptile are going to love this," chuckled Rick, "you may want to cage your beast, the Jacksonville zoo!"

"You're kidding, I'm sure!" retorted Joanna.

"Not at all, you'll be taking up steel bars for cages, along with special reinforced doors, dry box style of course; drop date three days time. The return is already scheduled. For that you will need to turn on the reefer, for that delivery. Pick up next day then the delivery in three from there. A easy trip of 2600-700 miles or about by the pace miler." replied Rick, proud to have it down pact ahead, "pick up the trailer number 7792 at the usual and leave yours."

"Great I'll leave later on tonight and take it easy with Sara and Solomon on the way," she exclaimed thanking her lucky stars for a good trip like that for her maiden voyage with the Sara doll. "Pays well I hope for my 80%?"

"Of course love!" and Rick quoted the prices round trip.

"Count on this wild trio to be at the zoo on Wednesday Rick, I'll call you as usual, bye," Joanna closed the line.

As always the excitement of the trip grabbed her. The challenge of the road plus the race to be there on time made her blood hum. The love of her job filled her as she began to routinely in her mind make a list of things to do to get ready before leaving. She automatically added in the extras for her plot.

The phone began to ring again. Joanna grabbed it before Solomon could make it from the far corner of the room. She looked at the number before answering. Smirking to herself, she read Brian's number.

"Brian, humph," She thought out loud with satisfaction was already getting worried, great.

Letting it ring, she dropped it to Solomon's joy on the bed. He immediately began his attack again as she left the room to take her shower. The ringing stopped after about seventeen rings to soon begin again, stopping after another round of seventeen. Finally it was silent.

Solomon tired after such a long battle was scratching at the bath to get in the shower with her. He looked up as if begging for help.

"Have a good time Sol," Joanna asked lifting him over the edge as she rinsed off the soap, "Cool down some, than we'll eat to celebrate someone's discomfort!"

Solomon loved the rain rooms; furthermore this one did good after such a long scrabble with the ringy ding thing he thought. He kept an eye on mistress as she moved to keep out of her feet's way, keeping his tail from being stomped on in the small bath.

These things accomplished, Joanna decided since he had already relieved himself to forgo Solomon's walk. This would save time to do the shopping, as well as the other stops she planned. Besides the little fellow was tuckered out plus falling asleep almost as he ate.

First stop, dressed as Sara, was to Sara's financial institution where she checked her master card balance making a payment. Joanna withdrew money from Sara's personal account with the debit card knowing the nip; it was her name with only one n. She than went to the counter to transfer all the money from one account to another. Sara's personal account to be exact, which Brian had access to via debit card to one he had no access to in any way manner or form.

Her story was she'd decided to close that account. Smiling confidently at the clerk she signed Sara's name without hesitation. That too had been a game between the twins, imitating each others handwriting and signatures perfectly. Since primary school to be exact, when even the teachers had trouble telling them apart or their homework. Sara had been good in mathematics, history, as well as science; so she did those home works and tests. Joanna was better in English, French, and geography, so she took care of them. The sisters switched classes to do the tests and exams when possible. It was a great laugh between them that was never found out so good were they at impersonating each o t h e r.

This devilish money business deed done, Joanna went back to her camper to transform into herself. Next stop was the supermarket to stock up some for the trip.

She much preferred her comfortable jeans and sweatshirt style along with her long clipped on braid to all the fussing of more womanly attire. Joanna did however, get a high imagining Brian when he went to withdraw the next time. Poor lad, he just lost access to about fifty thousand dollars. Of course, this would render impossible his capacity to declare Sara missing. Furthermore in any way claim insurance policies. His dreams must be slowly souring now.

Having well thought this over, she was happy with herself as she said, "We are getting to him Sara," as if Sara could hear her.

Taking her time she carefully chose foods that would not take too much space, keep fresh the longest, along with canned goods to eat cold. This time she had not had her usual cooking spree at Sara's before going on a trip. She went to the pet shop to stock up on Solomon's food pellets, supplements, and vitamins. Joanna was captivated by a small medallion chain collar. She purchased that along with a snazzy leather vest, and more litter.

Her shopping, including her calculated mind bending deeds done, she drove back to the apartment. To tell the truth she was quite satisfied with herself plus the events of her day so far.

Chapter 6

RUNNING WITH LITTLE SISTER

THE TRUCK WAS packed with the chosen food supplies, plus the needed clothing and accessories for herself, including Solomon. Naturally all were properly chosen as well as placed. She'd of course taken into consideration the climate change between Quebec and Florida. Joanna passed the vacuum in the truck, doing a quick cleaning of the dash, windows plus the gages. In order to fill out the paperwork she verified and inspected the truck and trailer. This was done to not only enable filling out the paperwork which stated her rig's condition but it was also a law to be obeyed or pay up big time. Road checks were often made concerning theses papers, so best to have them properly filled out and to date within the allotted time slot. Next for she prepared her bills products carried last trip, the papers used for in or outbound export/ import, along with her logbook and inspection papers to also give to the dispatch at the companies' terminal. These aspects of preparation done she returned inside to finish up preparing the apartment for her absence. Little things like doing out the litter box, checking what was in the refrigerator to see if it would keep as well as in the pantry. She folded her wash to then begin to prepare the Sara doll's pack sac. J.J. ate a quick late lunch cum supper then washed up the dishes. Taking her shower to get rid of the days grime, she let Solomon play in the tub for a bit again. All this done it was now almost one p.m. Time to get the doll in the truck.

Joanna wrapped the doll folded in two in a blanket so it would look like she was just taking out bedclothes. She left it in the sleeper for now till later when she was ready for it. For now she began to prepare for it as she threaded the metal eye hooks with fishing line and put her wrist bands attached to one strand each. J.J. then laid them upon the dash leaving the other ends free for attaching onto the dolls rings through the prepared hoops. Of course, once the doll was installed minor length adjustments would be needed. This she would do on a stretch of a back road which was hardly ever traveled before hitting the more traveled routes. Off she went then to fetch Solomon, having started the truck leaving it to turn over to warm up before setting out.

Solomon knowing the routine, was anxiously waiting beside his leash on the sofa. He was fearful mistress would take off again without him as she had done for her shopping expedition. He was wearing his new chain collar necklace with the medallion and sporting his new vest. A handsome yet comical sight, for he made Joanna remember herself waiting for a date who was late, wondering if they'd forgot or decided not to show.

As soon as she sat upon the sofa you can be sure Solomon was on her knee and in position to be leashed or dressed. It was his way of saying," glad you could make it, can we go now, Love to ride!"

Loving to ride was an understatement, he adored it. Of course, he would now share his seat with the Sara doll. To tell the truth nothing really new, for when the real twin had come, he had done so with no difficulty, furthermore with good grace. It would be odd to ride however with the doll, since the truth was a painful fact, as well as recent and a solitary knowledge. Nevertheless if she wanted to achieve her objectives it was part of the plan that had to be done as convincingly as possible.

The last couple of days she had come to accept the fact that to share her life with Sara, having her beloved twin looking over her shoulder was no more. Joanna was sort of on automatic pilot, with her destination plotted out depending on the circumstances and events as to which way to go about things. Yet, the goal, or final achievement was well defined in her mind. It was simple, and plain. She was going to make Brian suffer, squirm, wonder, worry, fear, and ruin his dream of yet another health club. She would conserve the Miller's money for which he killed, in the Millers pockets. He would pay! Maybe not in jail, yet anyway, but in sweat, and tears if not blood for depriving her of her beloved twin.

As she pondered the many details she had to take into account, the facts of Sara's life were now very important to keep her existence to others as real as possible. J.J. thought of yet another point. Good thing the trimester of the mill had just finished as well as all the accounting, and government papers that had to be done for that period. It gave her about two to three months loose if needed. At the last heard, Sara, who had an office at home doing work for small companies, had not had any new clients which suited her fine. Sara, being the person she was, had fixed it to work like a madman with the trimesters all at the same time so as to have spare time and freedom to travel and so on. This too suited Joanna well. Leaving some points that could lie without notice or bring up suspicion on her plans. Sara's assistant had been notified of his patron's taking a vacation. He had confirmed all would be well, and that he would take care of the usual preparations as well as his other tasks. Joanna had at the financial institution fixed it that his salary, office rent, along with all utility bills, and so on like payments would all beautomatically deposited without fuss nor the taking of her busy time into the proper accounts. This of course worked both ways, giving her more time along with ringing a few bells. Brian would take notice that all was kept up to date as the norm. Except Sara was not as normally by his side or by hers. Nor did he know her plans; after all she was supposed to be dead, possibly mysteriously disappeared. Just as though it was sadly true it must not show up in life to others that way.

Coming out of her deep river of thoughts, she realized Solomon whom she had been petting had fallen asleep waiting. The truck also had waited. J.J. would have to fuel up on the way. Instead of putting on his coat or leash, she stuffed them in her pocket. Picked up her beloved pet cuddling him inside her jacket she did the short walk. Awake now, he didn't mind this at all, it felt good to him. Cuddled up to her neck he basked in her warmth tasting her smell. Hanging on like the lizard he was, as she turned out the lights locking up before leaving. At last, they rolled out of the driveway now technically on their way.

Having switched trailers, given in, plus received her paperwork, Joanna, headed for the particular stretch of back road she had in mind. Here she would finish installing her Sara doll. Just a few minutes later It loomed ahead. She pulled the truck to the side after confirming that there were no curious onlookers to watch as she set things up. Coast clear she got out of the driver's seat.

Solomon looked on questioningly, as if to say, "Already, what's up Mom, we got a problem?" as he crawled down from his regal position of king of the castle upon the headrest. He scooted to the back where Joanna was unwrapping the doll. If iguanas could smile, he did. Seeing the doll, in his little mind meant his favorite treat, cheese. He waited till Joanna put the doll in the passenger seat and had installed the seat belt. He placed himself at the foot of the doll patiently waiting. Looking at

Joanna with great expectations, he put his forehand on the leg as if to chug her memory.

Joanna intent on tying the fishing line to the dolls hoops leading from the rings, at first did not catch on to the subtle demands of her pet. As she bent down to get the scissors, she saw him. Immediately she noticed that particular attitude with the tongue flicking in and out as if trying to talk. Knowing him as she did, it didn't take much to figure out what he wanted. Chuckling she went to the refrigerator to get a piece of cheese. She put it on the Sara doll's shoulder, admonishing him that she hoped it would not become a habit with him all the trip through. Joanna would definitely end up with an overweight, constipated iguana.

This done, Solomon was content to munch on his widened padded perch. She set back to work in the waning light of that day. The doll positioned properly once set up looked pretty good. Joanna sat herself in her seat putting on the wrist bands which already had their lines attached. She began to practice on how the doll moved in accordance to her movements. Having made a few minor adjustments in the length of the line she had it down to a fairly workable comfortable apparatus. When she lowered her right hand the left arm of the doll lifted. When she lowered her left wrist the doll seemed to wave with its right hand, lifting it to be seen by outsiders. Yes this wasn't bad at all she thought to herself pleased. Having had the foresight of lowering the air pressure in the air-ride seat, the doll hopefully should move slightly with the motion of the truck. Driving a piece on the rough road she saw that it did. The only thing a bit odd was, when she shifted with her right hand the doll continuously held its arm up. Parking, she tried her next idea. Taking off the right hand wrist band and fastening it to the steering. No, this didn't turn out well, for each time she turned the wheel the doll seemed to point at something. Brain wave, she fastened the band to the trailer air evacuation pull or push knob after adjusting the lines length. Now, when she wanted to move that arm, she just tugged discretely upon the line to the desired height while driving the truck with her left hand. This worked perfectly. J.J. now had without hindrance her independent mobility to shift, plus work the dash controls, and the capacity to simulate life to the stuffed creature beside her.

Solomon of course watched the whole procedure thinking humans were even stranger than he believed them to be, but he loved her anyway. This thing that moved every so often was sturdy, offering him a more secure perch while allowing him to still watch the road. To top it off, this thing had perfumed hair to cuddle, less silky than mistresses, yet better than none. Yes he was a happy iguana, even if mistress was a bit strange lately.

It was now late afternoon, early evening as Joanna pulled into the fuel island at the flying J in Vaudreil. She quickly tanked using her J card to help things along faster. Once having been to the fuel desk to salute Adelle she took her free glass of hot chocolate. J.J. then hurriedback to her truck. It had gone smoothly so far. Putting back on her wristband she pulled out heading for the 401 highway. She planned to cross over into the state of New York at Landsdown border entry, otherwise known as Watertown New York or Thousand Islands. Then she was to cross through that state on the 81 to Pennsylvania as the beginning of her route to Jacksonville Florida.

Joanna and Solomon thus began their run with the stuffed Sara doll sister. They headed down the black ribbon leading them yet again to new horizons and into the unknown yet vaguely defined future. The joy of exploring new places each and every way possible melded with her dream of getting even with Brian Thorp.

Joanna loved being a professional driver. The company she hauled for satisfied her so far and paid on time. Her dispatch most days could be fun, even likeable. The trips answered the needs of a widespread varied clientele so it was not monotonous. She along with Solomon enjoyed their freedom, as well as the everyday challenges. Their lifestyle was in a way a vocation; to them it was the blood humming in their veins, and they both seemed to thrive on it. Now though, the adrenaline was even more amplified, driven by yet another addiction besides trucking.

That of getting even. Each minor step achieved towards this gave her a thrill that she, a good little girl had never felt before. My how she was changing.

"God help me not to go overboard," she silently prayed before shifting forward into the line of duty.

They began their run in a shared solidarity of thought. Joanna automatically controlling her rig as she planed her next moves had an expression of determination. Solomon had a look of joyous wonder plastered upon his twinkling eyed face. While the Sara doll held a secret smile as her vacant eyes stared on ahead.

Solomon upon his perch watched everything, his tongue flicking the air tasting the stressed atmosphere. This put his mind on alert to protect mistress along with his territory. He couldn't deduce what was wrong, but all his senses told him things were different. He ordered himself to look, listen, to be on full alert and guard. This reptile now also had a mission.

The Sara doll sat there with its painted lips curved in a slight smile. The dolls mindless eyes reflected the passing lights and scenery, moving ever so slightly with the motion of the vehicle, a mockery of what was once sacred.

The Pete purred as the turbo whistled its song of powerful strength. It silenced every now and then to let the rumble of the Jacob brakes growl its displeasure. That of holding back its unleashed muscle of the big dogs. All eighty thousand pounds gross weight rolled majestically down the highway.

Running with little sister had not turned out to be what it should of been, however, Sara's memory was alive within the vigilantly twin if not in the stuffed image.

Chapter 7

SOWING THE TRAIL

At Wilkes Barre, Pennsylvania, Joanna began to feel the weight of the hours. It was now a bit past midnight, she had covered about four hundred miles apart from her other activities. Heavy eyed she rubbed the back of her stiff neck before beginning the process of downshifting to slow the rig. Having not stopped since the border, Solomon along with J.J had munched upon the prepared food left within arms reach. Sandwiches, cheese, chips; all topped off with various cookies washed down with a few bottles of juice or water to take away their hunger.

Solomon had had fresh lettuce, a bit of cabbage, along with cheese to accompany his food pellets kept in a dish just inside the sleeper. He had had his water dish uncovered a few times during the ride to quench his thirst.

He was now perched eyes closed upon the lap of the Sarah doll. His head weaved in a continual yes motion by the slight rocking of the moving rig. He seemed to confirm his mistress's thoughts, "yes she'd done enough for today, yes they were worn out, and yes it was time to stop, yes it was time to sleep, yes to anything just let me rest!"

Totally agreeing with these imaginary confirmations she pulled into a rest area. Joanna rapidly spotted a space to park her rig between a broker and a M.D.D. Transport truck.

She straightened out her rig verifying the solidity of the shoulder cautiously. Having parked to her satisfaction, not hindering the space to allow the traffic flow nor the eventual leaving of the other rigs; Joanna heaved the parking brakes.

The hiss of the compressed air alerted the dozing iguana who licked his lips seeming to smile sleepily. Sol blinked his question to Joanna, "We get to go to bed now?"

"Yep, time to hit the hay boy, I'm bushed!" Joanna replied to his silent question. She toggled the switch to lock the doors. Next J.J. bumped the idle up to the desired R.P.M.'s, then switched the heat on full to warm the interior for their down time.

Dimming the headlights, she left just the parking lights on, closed the slightly ajar window on her side for safety sake. Then after undoing the wrist band she slipped off her work boots. Oh wiggling her toes felt so good after the long confinement of her footwear plus the continual pressure of the pedals. The tightly muscled calves began to relax. She had been so stressed the last days these unusual cramps decided to show their ugly face to her misfortune. Standing she gleefully stretched in the hi rise cab. Turning into the sleeper, she picked up odds and ends of their snacks from the floor, dropping them into the garbage bag. Flicking the heat control switches for the sleeper she adjusted the flow of the warm air to a comfortably low temperature for their sleep time. Stretching back into the cab she lowered the heat flow there to minimum, scooped up the weary waiting iguana to set him upon the lower bunk with her. Closing the leather curtains to give intimacy for undressing, she took a quick visit to the loo to at last lay down to succumb to sleep.

Finally, reptile alongside human sank into the welcoming foam mattress. Joanna cuddled into the sleeping bag while Solomon hugged the braided hair piece he had sneaked off the shelf.

Suddenly Joanna sat bolt upright, "Hells bells!' she exclaimed, pulling her weary body out of the bunk.

Solomon had pounced to the edge, tail poised, tongue flicking with a mean look in his eye. He searched for the reason of Joanna's abrupt actions.

Joanna turned on the light to comfort her pet, "Forgot the Sara doll!" she told him giving his sides a rub to calm the frustrated iguana. He in turn looked disgustedly at her.

His head shaking with his warlike outstretched beard seemed to say "Shit lady, you scared the living daylights out of me!" but he forgave her rubbing his chin on her arm before returning to his nesting place. "Yep, humans could be weird, but useful," he thought before falling back to sleep, "Good thing this iguana was here to take care of this one!"

Joanna opened the curtains after slipping on her shirt, down on her hands and knees she went to get the doll. Untying the fish line she freed it, hauling the stuffed fake unceremoniously into the sleeper with her. Closing the curtains she than lowered the top bunk. Hugged the doll like a much cherished toy as she sighed, J.J sprung a leak letting a lone tear roll down her cheek. Swinging the doll into the top bunk, Joanna remembered to set the alarm clock. Again she lay down once more. Switching off the light her last thoughts yet again were of Sara as she sank into much needed sleep.

Six thirty the alarm buzzed. It got its usual swat, Sol his permission granted for his morning cuddle, while Joanna took her usual ten minute lay about. She then shifted herself into gear. J.J. improvised a quick body wash from a margarine dish of soapy water with a face cloth. She took another for rinsing. Joanna dried herself off to then dress after making up the bunk. Having made the bed she found her hair piece, which thanks to the reptile needed to be combed as well as braided once more.

Now neatly done she clipped it on. Sol got sprayed with distilled water she carried, to help hydrate his skin.

They both ate prior to putting on their outdoor clothes against the outside temperature. Joanna did her inspection whilst Solomon did his relieving himself. Solomon was set back in the cab. Joanna went to the ladies room offered in the rest area; there she emptied the loo cleansing it for future use. She washed her hands to then give a quick call to her Dispatcher previous to heading back to the truck.

Upon her return, she met up with another trucker she knew with the handle name Slingshot. His surname came to be because he had once accused his Dispatcher of aiming and firing him in undesired directions. Thus he was christened slingshot by his peers and it had stuck. Taking a few minutes to salute him, they exchanged news. J.J. made sure that exchanged news. J.J. within the short conversation she had let out Sara was with her. They wished each other a good haul, than returned to their duties.

Joanna could hear the cell phone ringing as she approached the truck through the crack of the open window. She hurried to unlock climbing in.

Solomon was busy whipping the damn thing which sat defenselessly in its stand. She read the number and ordered Solomon to back off. He did with bad grace, giving her an indignant look plus the evil eye to the ringy dingy. He felt it was his duty to lay low that screaming talking box that took Mistresses attention so.

Taking a breath she answered with her usual, "J.J. here."

The voice on the other end made her skin crawl as it cheerfully said, "J.J., how ya doing, big bro. Brian here, is the love of my life with you?"

Turning white than red with anger, she fought to control her voice before answering.

Noting the hesitation Brian inquired, "J.J., you still there, bad connection or what?"

"Brian, Sara doesn't want to talk to you now. I don't know what you two lovers are quarrelling about this time; she won't say. But she is real mad with you. You are well in the dog house now boy!" replied Joanna in a slightly wavering voice feigning exasperation.

"Ya, well that's between us and she'll get over it, you know us, two passionate people."

Turning her tongue a few times before answering she replied, "Ya, between you two but." after a small pause she continued, "I love Sara, and I will always be there for her. We take care of each other, you know that. Another thing though . . . she has some marks on her face? Sarah said she took a fall and to leave it at that."

The line was silent for an instant. Then with a snort he came back, "Ya, she took a fall, but I haven't seen her since. So you see I wouldn't know what marks she has!"

"As long as those marks are not your having abused her Brian! Its cool with me lover spats, you get the picture big bro. Brian I'm sure. Sara is the sweet twin, I'm not!" bounced back Joanna half joking while totally threatening, yet one hundred percent forecasting his future.

"Well J.J, I have to get back to the office, tell Sara to take her time, I'll be waiting for her O.K.?

"Will do, but she said to not even mention your name for it made her sick to her stomach, like I said you are in the dog house." answered Joanna through tight lips.

"O.K., I get the picture, tell her anyway. Hey I'll call back now and then, she'll answer one day, bye!" he quickly hung up before anything else could be said.

For a moment she sat there holding the silent phone. Then she shut it off to slam it into its stand, "Dirty stinking two-faced dog" she screeched.

Solomon looked on pleased that mommy at last was giving hell to the ringy dingy thing too. She seemed to understand what a beast it was at long last. Things were getting more interesting.

Joanna squared her shoulders, and then got her rig moving. It was back to business, save for her mind buzzed with unladylike names for her brother in-law. Solomon settled upon the arm of the passenger seat for the first leg of the journey. He was enjoying the sunshine upon his body. Yes he was a content iguana. Sol was especially pleased with mistress's falling out with the ringy-dingy.

A few hours drive into the day the pair turned off into Carlisle Pa, to fuel. J.J. took time to pick up a few things at the J store to chew on during the rest of the day after giving a call to her friend Daveda. She had entered the J store as Sarah using her company card to pay for the fuel, but Sara's credit card for her all other purchases. This included two matching T-shirts with; "Pennsylvania? I was there," marked on them.

Back in the truck she installed the Sara doll now wearing one of the new T-shirts as she herself was. Solomon took his place upon the Sara doll's shoulder. He relished the feel of the hair, making himself comfortable for the next leg of their journey. Basking in the strengthening morning light, he noticed that his water dish was close by but no food had been set for him or his mistress. His logic told him they would be stopping for next food time. Secure in his comfort along with this hopeful knowledge, he settled down listening to the animated voice from the audio book which was playing.

About three and one half hours later they pulled into Carmel Church Flying J, Virginia Plaza truck stop. Joanna, after finding a parking space put on Solomon's leash in order to take him for a walk. Once upon the grass, which was way warmer compared to Quebec, Solomon who enjoyed his nature walks spotted a real tree to his greatest delight! Scrambling up to the first branch he stretched out his full length with his tail comfortably hanging down. This spot allowed him to better observe the goings on around him. Registering the different reactions of passing people to his presence, he kept an eye upon mistress. She sat upon the curb lost in thought as she was smoked one of her rare burn sticks. The smell prickled his nostrils but it was a rare habit. Something was bothering her. How he wished she would climb the tree, stretch out to relax with him; it would be good for her. But no, she wouldn't.

Crushing out her cigarette, Joanna looked up at an approaching man. He was burly with a thick beard. He wore a red cap perched up on his shaven head. Recognizing him she smiled then waved to him.

"Woodchuck how you doing?" she saluted him.

"Pretty good, on my way back to the homelands," he answered with his strong French accent, while lowering his bulk upon the curb. Pulling out his pack of DuMaurier cigarettes, he offered her one which she refused, he continued, "The usual, brought up a load of wood to Florida now heading back with machinery on the flat bed," he chuckled his remarkable way which was the reason for his handle name; that along with fact he always hauled wood flatbed style.

Once having chewed the rag for about another ten minutes, Woodchuck left after telling Joanna to give his best to Sara. That is when the lazy critter hauls herself out of the sleeper. He joyfully went his way still chuckling abouthis own words.

Joanna had gotten her reluctant iguana out of the tree. Now installing him in the truck after having fed him outdoors to his delight, she left. It was her turn to have her meal at the restaurant. At three thirty all had been done, once more readied for the next leg of their journey. Back on the I-95 they headed towards Florida.

Before leaving the parking, she as Sarah called Clara and George Tisson to let them know that she was supposedly with Joanna. She thus stilled any of their worries when too much time passed without news from the girls. She informed them that she was taking a prolonged vacation where she would figure out what she wanted to do concerning her marriage with Brian. She refused to say what the cause for the rift was, other than stating the need for time.

The Tissons in turn related the story of Brain's call. They told how he at first insisted they were hiding Sara. This of course had the couple worried. Not wanting to infringe upon the twins private life they had chosen to await anxiously their weekly call. Now their fears relieved they respected Sara's decision. They sent their love to Joanna who according to the story was taking her shower in the truck stop.

It was not pleasant to pull the wool over the Tissons eyes. They were dear to the twins; however, Joanna didn't want them to worry. Just as she did not want them to be too involved in the intricate weaving of her web.

Johanna knew her prey was sly, heartless, as well as single-minded, so she had to play her cards right. By answering the phone to speak to Brian she had not only put him on panic, but unknowingly helped his similar decision of vengeance to fester. Now he too was out to get them. Furthermore he had started the machinery of his own deceptions, as well as detections for his own private hunt.

Five and one half hours later, still on the I-95 after a ten hour total driving day, they pulled in. Weary with tummies protesting in growls of hunger they entered the Latta South Carolina, J truck stop. Though tired, the pangs of hunger gnawed, so she went to get two take out meals at the Dragon oriental counter. She had a fresh mixed vegetable salad prepared for her vegetarian Solomon of course.

They ate listening to the radio softly playing retro rock, as Joanna sang along with the better known tunes. Solomon loved to listen to mistress sing as he lovingly watched her pick up the remnants of their supper. Evening rituals done; such as the tour to relieve himself while Joanna verified her load checking the tires, their day at long last was truly complete.

They lay down to have a well deserved sleep within the interior of their home on wheels. The humming of many diesel motors both near and far, along with rumbling reefers here and there didn't bother Joanna. She was accustomed to these nightly lullabies. It was all part of her life, as much as a city dwellers hearing passing vehicles, horns, sirens and what not was theirs. However to her, these sounds were much more pleasant than the busy city sounds. To her ears, it was as if a murmuring army lay in wait, tensed, ready to attack the black ribbon eating up the day's challenges. Restlessly they obediently awaited the go of their drivers to bring their varied merchandises to their numerous destinations. Their runs answered the many needs of the wide and diverse population.

Many however, condemned the big Rigs on the roads seeming to despise their presence. Numerous people openly as well as verbally showed contempt with non-respect for the driver's needs or spaces by law recommended to enable them to safely maneuver theses steal monsters. Like spoilt children though, they were hasty to complain when the transport business came to a halt, ceasing their busy routines. This inactivity quickly touched their daily comfort resulting from their unfulfilled needs. Yes, it was a strange relationship between the people and the truckers. Drivers, in reality were a special breed of people living with ways, hours plus stresses non truckers couldn't imagine. Truckers,

J.J. thought did have too many rules to follow; unfortunately though not very many rules to protect them, nor their salaries, rates or other things most took for granted. Sadly however, countless uninformed people often judged drivers as being ignorant, non schooled or unable to exercise other careers. Yet this unlimited as well as wide spread family Joanna willing belonged to of truck drivers, was by free choice. Her degree in journalistic writing lay gathering dust at the family home. Her certificates hung in her room where the Tissons proudly guarded them as part of the twins past.

Joanna along with Solomon awoke rested before the alarm went off. Having fed her pet, Joanna hauled out Sara's jewelry box finding what she had been searching for.

Her twin true to form had not been wearing the real diamond engagement ring, or the fancy matching engraved wedding band that dreadful day. Sarah feared loosing or whatever the real ones, so she had had a fake set made. J.J. had always felt it was more a fear of Brain's gambling habit; thus them ending pawned to pay a debt. The imitations were well made and they had even fooled Brian to this day.

Not knowing or truly caring about all his wife's activities; this was but yet another little untold story he never knew about. Sara would had loved to of shared more of herself with him for the little things in life added up to be big things. Save for having quickly realized his game of indifference to such details, she had adjusted labeling such things as of non importance or priority in their telling of them. Though Sarah, her twin suffered much sadness due to things of this sort; Joanna knew for a fact that at times she felt that Brian didn't really know her. Furthermore, stating how good it was that she had Joanna to share life's details with fully proved the point.

Feeling slightly dirty, she slipped on the set of rings, disliking the attachment it made her feel Sarah had with her murderer. She found it distasteful. Yes, that what should of symbolized love filled with respect, along with caring and support to spawn happiness till death did they part; had in reality been a ball and chain. A dragnet that had towed her devoted twin to a watery grave by a pure thoroughbred hypocrite who had promised to do her good!

Seven am. Joanna as Sarah was already in the shower enjoying the feeling of washing away the trails dirt as she cleansed her short hair. The lady at the fuel desk when she had had her shower deducted from her J card had remarked on what a lovely set of wedding rings, as many did when the showy, flashing diamonds caught the least rays of light sparkling with vulgar pride. She had taken much caution with her makeup including hair styling, donning Sarah's clothes, plus mimicking her ways. She left the shower room to order a cheese omelet for her breakfast. Being friendly with the waitress and using her hands to punctuate her words as she knew were Sara's mannerisms, the ring danced catching attention again.

Back at the truck around eight thirty a.m., she unpacked Sara's souvenir shopping for the Tissons. Gladly putting the rings back in their box she changed into her clothes. The braid was clipped on and hair flattened out with a bit of gel in it to give a heavy look. Next she got her pack sac ready to carry her pet clandestinely in for his shower in the next episode of her deception.

Joanna next placed a well chosen proportioned box in the bottom of the Pack sac. This was specifically kept for this very reason allowing shape and form to the bag in which Solomon could freely move without smothering. Installing then his baby blanket in the bottom brought a certain iguana to attention. The owner of the said blanket waited, visibly excited as he joyfully stood swinging from side to side. He knew what this meant, something to look forward to, "His turn in the rain room!"

Joanna took off the small piece of material held in place by Velcro. This gave way to an opening in the box near the bottom plus a tight mesh pocket outside. This to the onlookers was an everyday pack sac in appearance. Though in reality it was a way to keep the pet in plus get him in, without being noticed. Just one of Sara and Joanna's fun things they did together to overcome or answer needs. In this case they had adapted the pack sac together. Oh, how they had laughed more than once at their and Solomon's secret. Everything ready wee Solomon joyfully crawled in knowing that he could peek out while having his ride unseen by onlookers upon his human.

Once settled into a cabin the waitress who had served her while she was impersonating Sara almost dropped the menu upon seeing her. Having quickly ate her toast; she tipped the server, and went to pay her bill. She again explained she had an identical twin as she chuckled with the stunned cashier. She spoke of her twins' earlier visit, and the reactions of the waitress and clerk. Laughing they said their good byes as she left.

Ten Am., Solomon tied to the bumper; she inspected the rig, checked the liquids levels, and once again filled out her log book. At ten thirty they were on their way again leaving a trail of credit card payments, and witnesses to Sara being with her, for Brian to trace.

Back on the I-95 about four and a half hours later they pulled into the Brunswick Georgia J truck stop. It was just an hour's drive from the zoo in Florida where she had to drop her load. Calling the zoo to verify the drop time of six p.m.; she was pleased to hear the confirmation. It was best at that hour for zoo visitors would be less a bother both for her and them. She than checked in with her dispatcher. She confirmed everything was on go. Rick, in turn relayed the news that early tomorrow he would give her her schedule for the rest of the ride.

Realizing the drop would have many close spectators who would discern the fact that the doll was indeed a doll, and far from being a human being, she made another decision. Joanna did not want to bring suspicion upon her carefully planned ruse, nor answer unwanted questions. So Sara allegedly had stayed back at the truck stop while the Sara doll got tucked away in the back.

Solomon sat upon the head rest of the passenger seat tightly gripping the velvet with his long nails. He was getting accustomed to riding the more comfortable Sara doll. To boot he was slightly miffed with mistress who had forgotten to put the armrest down to his dismay. Shortly into the ride she remedied this however, gaining her pet's pardon.

At the zoo Solomon was the star of the show, of course he loved it. People here didn't fear nor hesitate to touch, rub, cuddle or pet him. He was welcomed, treated with due respect for his kingly appearance wearing his new vest with the medallion on his collar, Strutting, fanning his beard, while posing he gained their admiration. Joanna looked on enjoying his antics laughing along with the workers and zoo keepers who came to see him.

Snapshots were taken by onlookers as well as to post on the zoo's bulletin board. She was for awhile herself again, forgetting for a moment the overhanging cloud of what she had taken on. Accomplishing her duties, surveying the unloading while consulting the packing lists to be sure all was as should be, with no errors having been made, time flew.

Her bills now signed all seemed in order, she carried out her scam. J.J. purchased a few stuffed toys, postcards plus a back scratcher in the form of a monkey with outstretched hands. She claimed these were for her twin who was waiting for her at the truck stop. Which was something

Sara did do often when she dropped a load near enough to a stop or a shopping mall, or when she was to return afterwards. Of course she used Sara's visa card, whichpayments were automatically once a month deducted from a healthy bank account. The statements would then of course by post be delivered to Sara's home. There Brian would surely verify these to check up on everything.

Back at the small apartment Joanna having a few days off went about her business. She had mailed the souvenirs to the Tissons enclosing postcards signed Sara, and even a snapshot of Joanna and Solomon at the Florida zoo, stating on the back, "Sara and Sol."

Sitting pensively in the small front room cum kitchen she now reminisced over all that had been accomplished during her Florida trip. Their return voyage had much resembled the going, where the sowing of the trail had continued. Surely this would prove fruitful in the near future as an alibi to Sara's lively presence and existence. Judging by the call she had received from Brian the evening last she now knew her course of action was taking toll. Yes blooms of deceit now flourished. She was certain her vigilant planning would bring forth a bumper crop under who's weight would make muscle bound not muscle brained Brian buckle. Force him to react, hopefully cause him to make a mistake that would show his true colors for all too at last see.

Chapter 8

TRIP TO CALIFORNIA

IT WAS ANOTHER November morning, human and iguana were in bed fast asleep. This Tuesday no alarm clock had been set. The tick, tick of the clock in the dimmed room could however be heard along with the soft snoring of Joanna. Footsteps petered, pattered in the apartment above. The sound of slightly heard traffic, in addition to the soft humming of the furnace could also be noted.

Solomon was the first to wake. He lifted his long body to check on mistress. She was still sound asleep so he figured he could do what he had to without missing anything. He crawled down from the bed b-lining it to his litter box. Taking a swig of water, he stretched. Looking around he found the room quite dark, yet he could hear sounds above. His muddled mind sought to understand, so he climbed his tree, jumped to the clothes box, then the window sill. There he forced his way through the space between window frame and the blind. At last he was where he wanted to be at that moment, up against the window itself. He watched curiously all that was going on, soaking up the sun. This satisfied him for awhile. Yet there was his basic instincts which told him hunger was getting to him. Managing to arrive on the other side of the blind once again without mishap, he sat on the sill for a moment. This iguana was thinking the situation out, and coming to a final conclusion. Why do it all over again by jumping down for a start to that square box wasting time and energy?

Then jump to tree, next blue earth, to after that climb bed to get mistress's attention? A lot of work he figured. Yes, when looking over the situation, he came to the speculation that he could do it in one jump. Meaning straight onto the bed, at least he hoped so. He would gather extra strength for his leap he thought as the solution. He began tightening his muscles preparing to spring. Yes, that way he shouldn't miss it he determined. Sol sprung with all his might. Truly a sight to see, this flying through the air iguana, and he landed. Right on mistresses belly!

"Oops," he thought as he was rudely shoved off by a very angry hollering mistress. First time he heard her scream that one at him. Good judgment along with survival instincts told him he had better hide under bed, which he wisely did.

Joanna, not even thinking of her ten minute lay about, jumped out of bed. Down on all fours she was after her pet, "Solomon you rascal get out of there, if you could speak I'd have you say you were sorry a thousand times!"

Solomon knew an angry human when he saw one, so he scooted a bit more out of reach knowing he'd stay that way till she calmed down. Just then the ringy, dingy started to sound off. He just couldn't resist that thing, so he did a death defying leap, to run between mistresses legs, dodging her attempted grasps to catch him. Then he rapidly climbed the bed, jumped to the night table to attack with enthusiasm.

Joanna's sense of humor got the best of her. She cracked starting to laugh at herself. This caused the busily whipping iguana to pause just long enough for her to grab the phone from him.

Solomon quit his whipping, jumping down to get another swig of water after all that. He scampered across the floor keeping out of mistresses reach, though she seemed to be all right now. Usually, when she made that crackling sound, it meant he would soon be forgiven again.

Hard being an iguana with so much to do in this human environment. If iguanas could sigh, he did.

"J.J. here," answered the wild haired lady iguana chaser.

"Rick here, are you ready to hit the trail again?" He questioned her.

"Depends on where, when, and how much my dear, my Pete doesn't work for peanuts, nor eat em, ha, ha," She laughed back.

"Oh ya, well San Francisco sound like a nice ride?" he continued on quoting prices, stating possible dates, the description of the load, covering all the details of the proposed trip.

After listening to these propositions she managed to wrangle an extra hundred dollars for the trip, so she accepted it. Hanging up she began to hum "San Francisco here I come," leaving the room to the wary iguana. She went for her quick morning wake up shower. Hmmm, thought Solomon, the rain room is working; therefore mistress must be in love with me again. So he skittered away to join her, begging to be lifted into the tub. He won.

Joanna, while munching on her late breakfast mentally ran down all the things she had already prepared ahead for the next trip. Being the type of person she was, almost everything had already been done. The truck had had its regular oil change, been greased, even the air filters had been changed according to her maintenance schedule. The liquids, meaning, windshield cleaner, prestone, and oil in the deferential had been verified as well. Air pressure in tires had been checked, along with the air tanks bled for keeping tabs on possible water condensation. Her tractor van had been cleaned, washed, and now sparkled. It was well readied, as well as partly packed. Cans of food, dry products, water, on top of Solomon's provisions were already placed on the shelves waiting for use.

The Sarah doll was in the back ready to go. All telling, what was really left to do, was prepare the clothing for herself plus the doll and tend to a few last minute things in the apartment. Not to forget of course Solomon. Then off to pick up her trailer which was already loaded with paper to deliver to a San Francisco envelope company or companies. So all in all she could leave shortly if she chose to. Her need for occupation made her choose that option.

Not on the job, the last few days had shown Joanna just how much her life had revolved around Sarah. She had found many hours filled with solitary emptiness.

Those down times not to long ago would have been filled with activities and laughter with her twin along with friends. She hadn't contacted their friends, for various reasons; therefore passing her time working or brooding in her apartment. She did not yet feel able to hold up the storytelling act of Sara being alive and well, in a face off with the loving Tissons. So visiting also had been out to the question just yet. Therefore, instead of her usual visit she had just called them.

Joanna dearly missed them, for the new void in her life would have been alleviated with a hug or someone to share her burden with. At times it seemed to be a crushing weight this knowledge, while suffering a lonely mourning. One thing she did know was in life we often had to make due with the hand dealt us, offered or picked up.

Sighing she pulled herself up from the table then began her routine duties. She figured she could pick up her trailer to hit the road by eleven thirty if all went well.

To tell the truth, the last few days had not entirely been non productive towards her present aim in life. That aim was of course setting up Brian to freak out, to even hopefully admit his dirty deed. The Pete was now equipped with a newly installed functional microwave which would help out in the meal department. J.J had found herself not feeling up to cooking ahead. Defeated by the emotions which overwhelmed her Joanna did not have the heart to do this now lonely activity. Before the tragedy it had been one of the much loved activities the twins had done together. So now it would be frozen meals bought on the way, canned goods heated up, or warmed over. This was all part of her new routine.

That is since Brian had let his lust for money and the financial realization of his California club drive him to murder!

Home baked goods would have to wait for awhile or till when she visited the Tissons' at least. This solution, with restaurant services would answer her needs for now, making her appreciate Clara and George even more.

Joanna was better at the wheel or with mechanical tools than kitchen utensils. With pots and pans, things seemed to stick burn or shrivel up when she was left to it by herself. So before she poisoned herself or Solomon died of smoke inhalation she had figured this was a cure for the present evil. Nuke everything that she was to eat on the road or eat cold.

Another devious pass time had been the buying as well as installing a new home desktop computer. She had also bought a portable one for on the road with a new speaker system which was a must. The truck had been outfitted for all this with a safe system to convert the energy to make them all work without shortage or danger. Cost a pretty penny but she donned it worth it for the completion of her charade.

She now had CD's she would play, home engraved and prepared with her voice imitating that of Sara. There she used the former twin's way with expressing herself and tones. These carefully marked CD's were mapped out to string conversations together or to but in resembling impulsivity. The accompanying sheets snapped to a dash clipboard for easy reading were to guide her choices of tracks. The Sara voice could then be found saying, possibly seemingly doing certain things, or even caught in the act of laughing or so on. All was ready to fit into cautiously controlled conversations. At times it was supposedly on CB, the phone, or be speaking to or with Sara for the benefit of certain people's hearing. Hopefully giving the realistic impression she was two twins not just one. Each CD was carefully labeled so by skipping from track to track she would be able to weave yet a new sham. This she sincerely hoped would give Thorpe the willies, hearing the voice of the wife he murdered. Hopefully capping all doubts, making him truly wonder what was up.

Joanna didn't regret any of her fraudulent actions where Brian was concerned, just what forced her into this situation. Sara's death.

By eleven the Pete was rolling out of the driveway as planned. Both iguana and driver were at their posts heading towards yet another piece of destiny. One good thing though; Joanna figured and planned she would get to see the sight of Brian's proposed new health club. The one he'd been blubbering about the last few months. Maybe she could even stake it out to learn a thing or two. At least destiny was taking her in the right direction. That is with this load to that state, if not having been kind to her she mused. She shifted into another gear starting towards her 12 day journey.

Solomon perched in his favorite position could tell it was going to be a long ride for his food supplies were bountiful plus there was an extra bag of litter under the bunk. He however was content to be once again in his mobile home. Sol found it much more amusing as well as action packed than the standstill one.

Yet he sure enjoyed the tree along with the nice rain room. However, he loved to ride watching the wonders unfold before him as he soaked it all in with mistress. In addition to it all this new stuffed look alike was quite comfortable. Things had been strange lately but interesting to this iguana.

Day four into the ride they were in Utah, where both driver along with pet enjoyed the warmer temperature. Solomon found that the white stuff on the ground looked a lot like the winter fluff that fell from the sky in cold time back home.

Mistress had however taken the time to get out here at a stop in Salt Lake City to take him for a walk to let him investigate that stuff. It was warm not cold, though it was crystallized, plus it didn't turn to water when licked but tasted like salt. It was all over, mixed in with sand that was warm to his belly. Sol loved to squish it between his fingers and toes. It was almost like a giant litter box, but clean every where. Beware he thought, either there was a huge iguana somewhere, or these people enjoyed this environment. He decided to stick close to mistress just in case.

They had restocked the food shelf when mistress had done her thing of switching hair styles plus going out twice a few times with and without him during the ride so far. Except today she seamed to be less in a hurry letting him discover more to his great delight. He loved it when she cackled at him smiling as he did his research.

Back in the truck Joanna had just finished doing her log book when the phone started to ring. Solomon was on it in a blink of an eye. He took to whipping it while scratching its leather casing which was really beginning to be quite tattered now after a 3 month trial of iguana attacks. She made a mental note to pick up yet another one for her pet to begin shredding. At last it was silenced; Sol the lone iguana swaggered back to the bunk compartment manly and proud.

Joanna grabbed the phone before it began to ring again knowing full well that all who were acquainted with her were aware of this strange ritual. They usually called back shortly after hoping Sol was a distance away while J.J. was close by.

Remarking the number displayed on the phone she first pushed the CD player into action. A miffed Solomon eyed her with his out of the reach enemy. He watched her as the phone rang again and Joanna cradled it to her ear. Yes, she cuddled it into her sweet smelling hair. Oh, this was one jealous iguana.

Shooing him away the CD players speakers now were filled with a joyous laugh as Joanna answered.

"Hello," she said as the background laughter died down.

"Joanna, hi, Brian here," the phone said as the CD played the supposedly Sara voice asking who it was?

"Brian." Joanna answered to the disembodied voice of Sara.

"Shit," answered that same Sara voice, than silence both in the cab in addition to on the other end of the phone.

"Guess she doesn't want to speak to me yet eh, where are you girls gallivanting to now?" he said in a so what voice.

"Well that's our secret," Joanna answered, "ladies time out on the black ribbon."

"Oh well, when the bills come in again, I'll know what you have been up too!" he said with a smirk in his voice.

"Gee Brian are you opening her mail?" Joanna asked innocently, as "Son of a Bitch," was exclaimed by the disembodied voice in the cab after Joanna had punched to another track on the CD.

"Well, thought I'd take care of paying the bills," he quipped back, "but then I discovered Sara's account at the Caisse Populaire de Montréal had been closed, so she'd better take care of it herself."

"I'll tell her Brian, but you know Sara always takes care of her bills as well as her responsibilities, so don't worry she knows what she is doing!" Joanna answered as a "Well," answered Brian, "she may not want to talk to me but she sure is bitching at me in the background there," he shouted back before slamming the phone down in Joanna's ear.

Pulling it from her ear making a face, Joanna's angry expression quickly turned to a huge smile. This was actually the first time she had ever enjoyed speaking to her brother in law on the phone she thought. Wow there is a first time for everything maybe.

"Hey next stop Nevada plus a bit of gambling. You want to see some more bills Brian?" She said out loud to no one in particular, "have fun opening the mail while watching what you hoped to spend be spent!" She said shifting her truck into gear as she head out.

Solomon, feeling the truck go into motion scrambled to his perch on the newly positioned Sara doll's shoulder. He was quite glad the ringy dingy was back in its stand. It to his joy no longer was cuddled to mistress's ear nor her flower scented hair. One day he would break through its tough hide spilling its innards, he promised himself. Nevertheless the thing seemed to regenerate its skin faster than an iguana could a new tail. He thoroughly disliked that thing, although he enjoyed the scenery unfolding before him. All this sand along with those weird trees appealed to him, as did the rock faced hills covered in bright sunshine. Yep he was a content iguana again, plus mistress seemed to be in good spirits too. Life on the road really was grand, for now anyway.

Day five into their trip Joanna was pulling into the gigantic parking lot of a Casino in Winnemucca, Nevada, not far from her entrance by highway 80 into Lodi, California. Here there was a great deal of parking space. It was all especially designed for big rigs, along with a good place to eat with plenty of quarter slot machines, game tables; the whole kit and caboodle all in one spot to boot. What was to most truckers liking also was they didn't expect you to be dressed to kill. It was a come as you are atmosphere where truckers among high rollers got to mix walking the same ground without judgment. All followed the same gambling rules for everyone was hoping to have fun plus win a little back.

Excited Joanna went into the back to pack her big canvas purse she had bought along the way, and of course on Sara's credit card. This plus other buys she had by internet banking paid out of first Sara's account, than repaid Sara's account out of her own account.

Jeepers, cyber space, internet and long distance banking was great. Wonder if they had thought of this particular possibility when they invented it? Nah, she said to herself, not everyone gets to be a vengeful witch on the hunt. Thank goodness, because hey think of the twisted world we'd have to live in. There are still some good people out there. Think of the Tissons she told herself. There is only one Brian Thorpe. S o . . . the sicko's were hopefully out numbered by the good guys. Hopefully that is with not too many Brian want to bees in comparison. She shrugged off her meandering and philosophical wanderings to continue her task at hand.

After feeding Solomon she took him for his short walk about to relieve himself. Joanna left the truck idling with the air conditioner on low. Though Sol loved the warmth she wanted to be sure he had fresh air circulating. Plus she did not want to have an overcooked, dehydrated reptile when she got back. All done and taken care of she got out leaving a sleeping iguana alone. She locked up heading for the anticipated fun, both present and future, real or imagined. Be it for herself or in the name of Sara's retaliation.

A good while later a cheerful Joanna with her big canvas purse bulging from the not so neatly as at first folded Sara costume unlocked the Pete pulling herself in. Solomon greeted Joanna doing his version of the iguana welcome dance prancing with joy on the floor. He looked eagerly up at her with his tongue flicking in and out excited to see her after her long absence.

Sitting in the drivers seat, she set the purse upon the other to reach down for her pet to cuddle him to her, "Missed me did ya, eh boy, always nice to be greeted by someone who loves you when we get in, and I love ya too boy! Guess what Mommy tried to spend some cash but won a package while in Aunt Sara's shoes, now won't Uncle Brian be on the edge when he hears of it. Especially the amount when the confirmation letter lands in by the home fax machine. I'd love to be a fly on his wall when that happens!" she said just before breaking up giggling like a drunken teenager.

The rest of the ride to the appointed drop according to this loyal and noble iguana seemed closer to normal life than it had been for quite awhile. Mistress was almost herself, even though sometimes he thought he was seeing double or flashing back now and then to repeated activities. Was mistress going senile or was he? No matter, he was content even if it may or may not be a fool's paradise; but it was with the one he loved. He puffed out his cheeks fanning out his beards in pride. He Solomon was honored to own his human along with the adventures they shared. He for one whole heartedly had no regrets belonging to his much loved mistress. Even if at times he found her strange even to him.

He couldn't pinpoint the exact why but he could sense the differences in mistress, see and feel her sudden mood swings. She sometimes went from cackling to rain-dropping. Whatever was bothering her, one thing for sure this iguana was going to stand by her.

Joanna, the drop now completed pulled up into a parking at the Ottawa Ca. truck stop. A nice surprise it was for she was able to secure a nearby parking to the main building. A luxury not often experienced by her, but much appreciated at this moment. The security here was considered to be very good. Mary-Ann a long time friend based in this very state had told her so. Therefore J.J. knew that if she left her truck for awhile it would be safe as well as its four legged passenger.

This security was very important, enabling her to scout on her own in less noticeable vehicle. For that is exactly what she planned to do . . . rent a car. Sol would stay with the truck. She intended to go have a look see for clues, maybe insights as to Brian's present situation. The location of the sight would not be hard to find due to his frequent blowing the horn about the wonders of its great corner placement upon two well traveled roads. One of his latest past times was stating the address, while strutting singing his own praises along with the sainthood of his Uncle who had made it possible. For Joanna, it was easy to remember streets along with addresses as well as major roads being in the line of business she was. After all it's a free world, she could go see where this costly wonders of wonders was landed in its progress of being created. Let's see what Sara had paid for with her life!

Chapter 9

ONTO THE SIGHT

SOLOMON LAY ON the dash fully stretched out sunning himself. He was totally satisfied with a full belly as well as plum tuckered out after playing with mistress. The gentle vibrations of the truck at idle massaged his underbelly helping him digest his meal. The morning sun was less intense than that of the scorching afternoons here. The evenings however he found cool. So Solomon simple creature he was in the morning staked out the dash, hit the back bunk for afternoon snooze, then choosing the passenger seat for the evenings. That is of course if the air conditioner wasn't on to high for his liking or dismay.

Joanna was in the back donning designer jeans, runners plus a hand painted T-shirt. She was walking again in Sara's shoes. So make-up was also a must for this escapade. She was at last getting the hang of it, doing the job a lot faster than in the beginning. Joanna, for example now managed not to jab herself in the eyeball with the eyeliner pencil as often as before. She could also brush on the mascara without smudging under or above her eyelids. The continuing problem was her holding back from fisting her itchy eyes, not being used to the eye makeup. This action obviously totally ruined it, making an awful mess only good for Halloween. The results being redo or repair which was both tedious plus time consuming which wore her patience thin. It was for her frustrating this thing of striving to look like a painted lady. One thing which had helped was her trading in the conventional mascara for a waterproof one, plus anti allergic makeup in Sara's tone choices. J.J. found this waterproof mascara stuck better, ran less, on top of smudging less frequently. Lipstick at least she was used to, able to do it in a blink of the eye. In her opinion make up was a waste of time. Lipstick though was acceptable to preserve her lips from becoming chapped.

Joanna emerged from the sleeper into the cabin where her lazy iguana dozed. The creature in question opened but one eye, blinked a hello or good bye, to fade blissfully back to sleep. She adjusted everything for the well being of her pet then got out of the truck locking up.

A rented car had been ordered. It presently sat in the car parking lot waiting for her use. The keys as pre arranged were to be picked up at the fuel desk. Off she went on yet another one of her adventures. J.J firstly planned to stop for a good meal, then shop. That done it would be off to snoop with a bit of poking around maybe. It should hopefully be an interesting and fruitful day she thought to herself.

Having a day layover was right up her alley. She hadn't even had to ask for a day off, yep destiny. She intended to make the most of it too. The Sara doll wearing Joanna's clip on braid laid upon the bunk simulating sleep with partly opened curtains for onlookers, to see. It served her pet also who could scoot into the back to his litter box if needed. Fresh water plus food had been laid out as well for Sol. A sign stood in the window saying do not disturb.

Joanna's step was light as she was eager to be on her way. She rushed to get the Ford Escort's keys. Armed with credit cards plus a false identity she set off to do her best or worse depending on the situation.

In the driver seat of the small vehicle Joanna felt out of place having always preferred vans, campers or wagons. These small cars being low to the ground tended to be ass bumpers while the seats folded you in two.

"Lord," she thought, "please do not let me get another back ache in theses little buggies!"

Weird as it may seem, she preferred her cars to be automatic though she was extremely capable of shifting as she had time and time again proven with her 18 double 0 Pete. However, for cruising the town along with bumper to bumper fun out of the line of duty she found automatic easier. But give her 18 wheels with a manual any day, rest assured she'd be happier than a fish in water. Trucks were tough though beautiful, good iron work horses, mastodons capable of carrying massive loads, so manual was a must in her point of view. The big dogs were for work and prestige which in itself became a game to the drivers who worked hard with and on their trucks. Yet upon the busy narrow roads, it was a lot easier to maneuver or find parking space for the Escort than for her Pete. Also in the Escort those ticket happy 3 wheelers weren't always on her tail waiting for her to stop so they could pounce.

Funny thing in this town trucks must drop their loads unseen, unheard of and heaven forbid parking, stopping or even hesitating for something to munch or have a leak. You stopped only to drop, other than that the trucks had to be on the move. The problem was more often then not your drop was not ready, contrary to your being so. Like a vulture you circled, waiting to land on your pray. Or you could say like a jet waiting for permission to land you kept going burning fuel. The only two means to justifying the standstill of the mastodons was to unload or if you had a breakdown. However, remember, be quick to get going as soon as possible in town or pay the ticket person big money for your offence.

Seemingly to the classy population trucks took space, marred the beauty of posh streets as well as hindered their going and coming of these influential high society people. Joanna had received one of those gifts from a sneaky ticket person who was hid in an alley catching her when she had stopped to ask directions. A gift she could have done without of course. No excuses were the bottom line of that person who seemed to take pleasure in signing their name on the ticket just before asking for J.J.'s autograph.

The upper classes tolerated the 18 wheelers just to get their stock, but had no knowledge or respect for the possible needs or expenses all that driving around curtailed. No get it to them, and then get out, with no thoughtfulness to what it may or may not take to do so, just as the comfort or requirements of the drivers were of no importance. Yet to put a 72-75 foot rig in ones pocket was impossible as well as doing a disappearing act to hide from those frisky 3 wheelers. Cash could well be part of those places for they seemed to guzzle cash quicker than you could say, "I'm having a heart attack!" while doing the unforgivable thing of being parked . . . Joanna snorted deliberating with herself.

That was city life in many places, but in California it was their way in the town of stars and idols. Long live the tourist flashing country for the stars, rich and famous.

On the outskirts it was more layback in addition to human, less rush or be run over. This disrespect, coupled with not being understanding, as well as the fuel waste due to time screw-ups, along with money exchange turned many truckers off of California trips. Joanna justified as well as reasoned to herself as she navigated the streets to get to her first stop, a gourmet restaurant.

Once there Joanna ate like there was no tomorrow, filling up on gourmet food including a huge steak. The waiter was amazed that such a small person could pack it away like so; the ladies legs must be hollow he thought. He knew many patrons who would like her secret allowing her to eat while staying slim. It was not as if she were a muscle bound butch either. She was a nice firm muscular shape yet a womanly form. This person was quite appealing though her manners could use a bit of polishing, as well as her idea of tips in a restaurant as such he thought.

Sitting back in her chair chewing on a toothpick Joanna wished she could loosen her jeans by unsnapping them. Heck, even unzipping a bit to allow her overfilled tummy space. She felt like she was chocking from the belly. Lord had she pigged out! She spit out the toothpick to then suck on her mint while waiting for the waiter to bring her fruit salad take out. The salad of course was to help Solomon forgive her for her long absence.

Usually buffets were her style and speed or fast foods on the road. But today was an exception to the rule. Sara loved gourmet foods; therefore Joanna figured she had packed away enough for two ladies. J.J both from hunger for something not in a can plus giving you know who a start when the bill came in. He would then see how close the girls had been to his sacred site.

Splurge was today's theme, which is just what she did in various upbeat boutiques. She allowed herself the many luxuries she usually denied herself. The holding back had not been from being unable to pay for them, but the fact she didn't feel a need for them. Joanna bought three sets of lace undies, even a dress she simply couldn't resist though she preferred her jeans. The predicament was still didn't know where she would or could wear that particular kind of dress. To the growing pile she had added a new bikini, sandals, short suits, tank tops, baby dolls, plus a few pairs of jeans.

Her favorite buy of the day was a floor length black leather coat along with over the knee laced boots to match. These she had always wanted for you could wear it with pants. Also the fact that she was a movie buff who had an affinity with the cool sexy actors wearing such things. In the past she had promised herself to one day own such a git-up. This promise was now kept as her other wishes would soon be to boot.

Of course this was real leather, with the price tag to match to her glee, real high. At any rate with the bundle she had won all this didn't even put a dent in it, so why not? Sara would have been proud to see her wearing some decent clothes instead of her forever every day duds.

Joanna at times when of dire need for a date in the past had simply ravaged her twin's wardrobe rather than go shopping. It was dress-up time for the girls all over on those few occasions and they had had a ball.

Yes she had many good memories to hold on to which either warmed her heart or steeled her for her many mind bashing Brian tricks.

Finally she jammed her last purchase into the trunk deciding she with Sol would dine on pizza tonight plus the salad. They would have a lot of unpacking to do placing these buys for easier traveling shall we say. She did a quick stop at a pizza shop, choosing two small pizzas rather than one big due to her micro wave's size. Joanna now was at last on her way to finally snoop. Poor Solomon must be beginning to think Mom abandoned the wee lad she mused.

Joanna had chosen to do her snooping just before nightfall after construction workers hours, not knowing at all what she would find.

This should make things less obvious, hopefully bringing less attention to her activity. Or so she had expectantly planned. Pulling out of the parking area she cruised along the highway set upon her present task. It was a short drive for the next exit was hers.

Turning left after the exit as her map studying of last night had showed, she did about one mile before coming to the corner of Fortunes drive and Economy lane. Just right there a great big sign, correction a huge sign, eye catching plus flashy like the owner proclaimed: "Soon to be another B.E.T. Health Center for all your health needs and dreams to come true!"

Well he did it, gotta give him that she thought, she now knew as well as believed you could shout, strut, and even brag even in writing.

So typical of that jerk Brian to seek the lime light even in a sign. There he was looking right at her from his self picture wearing a bikini male version of the G string with his muscles bulging in a sexy pose inviting both the young along with the old to not only dream of fitness but to attain their dreams.

She felt like getting a spray can to add a few lines like, "To what cost or price are you willing to pay, like till death do us part maybe?"

"Catty Joanna," she admonished herself. However her journalistic side was taking over as she began to imagine how she would have written up this person's endeavors, along with his financially supported accomplishments. She chose a parking space to slip into along the curb.

The B she knew to stand for Brian, the E for Egor and naturally the T for Thorpe. His slogan was: "Bet on yourself not your present health, join a sure spot for health development and maintenance."

Catchy the whole set up she did have to resentfully admit plus he did have the body if not the brains. Egor, she always thought would have been a more fitting first name for this person rather than Brian, knowing him as she did.

"Yep he'd fit into a horror flick she decided. A sexy monster would be a new angle now wouldn't it? She giggled to her self as she stepped out locking up.

Chapter 10

BEING SEEN

HAVING HAD SECOND thoughts Joanna unlocked the vehicle to climb back in. Once outside she had not felt too safe in this nearly deserted place.

Mentally shaking herself out of her nasty thoughts she began to take in the site itself. J.J. re examined the huge sign, wow he even had confirmed himself as a gassy ass she thought to herself. Written for all to see the sign advertised the opening for the 1st of November of that year. However, if anything this was far from being ready. It looked utterly abandoned except for the dimly lit trailer in the far corner. It was surrounded with piles of sewage and drainage pipes waiting to be installed. No heavy machinery or tell tale signs of present activity; just of past activity. The layout was riddled with lag along with wheel ruts crusted completely dry jutting up all over. Garbage littered here, there, everywhere attesting that once upon a time humans were here.

Pickets laid out where the promised building's foundation was to be.

Yet it was only partially dug out. A sure symptom to a sudden as well as undesired full fledged stop she figured. Interesting, very interesting, she thought as she peeked through her pocket binoculars bought just today.

Looking through them she could make out the person sitting in the trailer window. What she saw was giving her the willies for hells bells he sure looked a lot like Brian. The only difference was the hairstyle, odd, very odd.

Joanna was so intent on trying to figure out who the mystery person was in that trailer that she was completely unaware of her surroundings.

She did not notice a tall figure that came out of the bushes by the curb corner. This blond giant walked with the stealth of a big cat. When he bent to say hello through the open window J.J. jumped dropping her binoculars guiltily to the floor. He smiled at her as he flicked on his flashlight to sweep the interior of her rental.

Joanna nearly had a heart attack being caught, yet she was almost glad when she realized he was an officer of the law rather then Brian.

Flicking on a switch Joanna illuminated the inside of the vehicle while asking if this would help. She always tended to be sassy in these situations to her twins grief. She picked up her binoculars now easily found with the light on. Brazen as a bear picking the neighbor's berries she thanked him for his presence.

"What's wrong officer and how can I help?" she questioned while looking into two thick lashed deep-set breath taking green eyes she felt she could drown in.

The officer in question chuckled at her show of bravo coupled with her quick show of sass. He after all had seen all kinds in his line of duty, thought this little sex pot did take one of the cakes. Her strong unabashed attitude spoke volumes which he enjoyed seeing and hearing.

"Just wondering what a lady like you was doing on an abandoned construction site?" he drawled with a Texas accent while flashing a slow sexy lopsided smile cum grin that made Joanna's bones melt.

Gathering herself together both from the effect this stranger had on her as well as to tell her tall tale. J.J. drew air then began to play her game. The question was would he buy her bluff. Quite the gamble, but oh it looked like fun to be had in her solemn line of duty to Sara.

Totally lying was not her style, but she had planned to stretch the truth a bit.

"Well, can you not see I'm staking out the BET health club that was supposed to be in business here? Geese I really pigged out today Officer Gregory Armstrong," she said reading his name tag, "and I figured a work out would at least bring it down to piglet!" she added while batting her eyes taking in how his uniform hugged his muscled form. The complete picture was making her feel the full carnal animal attraction as dizziness spun her thoughts in other paths then her word game. Hubba, hubba, what a hunk of raw meat she'd love to cook!

He in turn well aware of the sexual current including the game listened for foul ups or other give ways in her explanation. Yet he was satisfied with her answer. Taking into consideration the female population, along with the male's to boot here were very hung up on appearances, not like the hard working rancher's daughters back in Texas.

"That explains the fruit salad from a gourmet restaurant!"

He quipped, "And why you can still sashay instead of roll!" he laughed taking in her feigned indignant look.

He bent down leaning upon the top of the car as he said, "True this place is way behind schedule plus it should have been opened by now. Problem is the owner ran into financial difficulties. Then the workers didn't appreciate back in August not being able to cash in their pay checks. That brings up the why I am here, to keep an eye out for folks who may be taking to vandalism or foul play. I personally deduct you fall into the harmless health nut category and or fan here.

O.K., you got your answers, now I ask you to please leave the premises, thank you very much." he said.

He was completely unknowing as to how true that remark was; all thanks to his generous filling her in with such delightful tidbits.

Joanna gave him the once over appreciating look as she smiled liking what she saw. He in turn stepped back from her car smiling back.

He waved his flashlight as if saying good-bye waiting for her to comply with his demand.

Joanna started the engine, waved as she put herself into reverse, resisting the urge to burn rubber as she left. To be stopped for that action by this particular male specimen who had a sense of humor, along with that heart pounding sexy voice . . . hmmm could be interesting in the least if not fun. Yet common sense told her to cool it, to not push to far nor tempt the tides of destiny. So she left peacefully though smiling like a star struck school girl or an idiot who just got a double D +.

Nevertheless she was still bothered by whoever that was in the trailer, plus wanting to get to know that peace keeper much more. After all, she had caught him too, looking down her blouse that is. So in her opinion they were both guilty she deduced as she took a last glimpse of him in the rear view mirror. Sighing she questioned herself about what a longer encounter would have amounted too. Friendship, going out; would it of been a taste of heaven or hell?

J.J. drove off to rejoin Sol. But her thoughts were definitely with the tall man she had left behind. As her Auntie M would say, "He could park his runners under her bed any day, anytime! Plus exercising horizontal style would be on the agenda; what a work out that could and would be for wedding bells to toll to."

Joanna wondered if his bedside manners were the same as his car side manners. Speculating about what rank he was, where he was from, if he was married or not as well as willing Joanna had switched unintentionally to automatic pilot once more. Her thoughts now lost in overdrive in a sea of new emotions, wrapped in silky sexual fantasy. All these feelings were new for this aged Sunday school girl. He sure looked capable of a blissful relationship she mused. He was strong yet fun, had a sense of humor yet was quick on his feet, as well as intelligent. Lord what a tempting tease that voice and body were. Her motions were robotic as she navigated the streets while her mind was fully occupied swimming the rivers of desire. What a change since Sara had been taken from her.

This reaction to a man was a first for her, chemistry she figured, electric currents she reckoned. Being twenty-five the unused wires were either faulty or overloaded.

"Ooh, was that her biological clock ticking?" she heard her self say, "Than let it tick!" she answered herself.

Though he was probably worth the pickup, as well as the road test, to be involved with a police officer now could prove sticky though sweet.

No for the present she had more important things to do as well as figure out. No time to moon like a lovesick puppy. School girl crushes didn't wear nice on a seasoned woman of twenty five. Sol was her companion while her Pete was the other part of her life.

Joanna was still scolding herself as she turned into the truck stop.

Chapter 11

CAT AND MOUSE

JOANNA WAS SO enthralled with the officer that she had not noticed the vehicle that had followed her to the truck stop. Nor the man who was now but a few parking spaces away leaning against another truck. He was observing her as she unlocked her Pete to get in after parking the Escort beside her van.

A certain loyal but impatient reptile also observed her as he watched from his look out point upon the dash. The door opened as he began to prance with joy greeting her. Sol jumped to her shoulder as soon as her waist had penetrated the door, cuddling her hair he held on as she finished her entry. Joanna gave her pet a head rub setting out a dish of the gourmet salad as a peace offering for her long absence.

Sol being a typical male played hard to get for about a minute or so. On the other hand, with just one flick of the tongue to taste the exotic fruits, he knew he had lost the battle. Incapable of resisting the dish he eagerly attacked it. Full of zeal the wee lad reminded her of her own meal to yet be had.

Hard to believe, but yep she was hungry again. Fantasizing was an energy pull she figured as her tummy growled. So she nuked a pizza.

Chuckling she watched her pet, hoping he wouldn't end up with an overloaded tummy as she had. Though he had no pants to inhibit him she figured he'd be shedding his skin soon if he continued so.

Her mind at last back on track she reminisced about what she had learned today. Yes dear brother-in-law was justly in a bind. His misfortune was truly her triumph, for Joanna had in fact foiled his plans. She was well pleased that a slice of justice had been rightfully served to the beast of a man. His dream as she had aspired had turned into a nightmare. Joanna personally considered his bloody deeds deserved much more when all was taken into consideration. Yes these discoveries partially soothed her hurting mind.

"God go get him, do not let him get away with it," she silently prayed, "your vengeance not mine."

Sol chomped gleefully as he watched Joanna, "The only good things about Mistresses long absences," he thought, "were her forgive me presents," he punctuated with choosing another piece to chew, "and oooh this was delicious! "Almost as good as cheese," he smacked his lips to underline his thought. "Yet, beware it will have the opposite influence upon my system," he chuckled to himself as he eyed the litter box.

While her pet happily chewed the succulent pieces of fruit Joanna unloaded her purchases, locking up again to go drive the car around to the car parking side. She expertly placed the Escort in a parking space up front, near the entry of the gas bar. As prearranged she took the keys to the fuel desk. There J.J filled out the awaiting papers, signing in the appropriate places to finish up by leaving the keys with the attending desk clerk. Deciding to get some fresh air to clear the cobwebs she chose to walk around the huge building rather than through it to her tractor van.

Grabbing a coffee on the way out she trotted merrily along towards her Pete breathing in deep the air and smells. She took pleasure in the sight of so many rows of trucks.

About a quarter of the ways to her eighteen wheeler she felt the hair rise on the back of her neck as the odd sensation of being watched set in upon her. She could feel hidden eyes boring into the back of her skull like hot coals. Joanna as Sara now not being the skittish kind turned around in search of the onlooker. She caught the glimpse of a red plaid shirt hightailing it between two dry boxes. That red plaid jogged her memory.

"The Brian look alike!" she gasped under her breath as she turned to resume her walk to the safety of her truck, "was he tailing her?" She wondered as she grasped her brass knuckle key chain in her fist ready for a fight if need be. few paces before her parked in a well lit spot, both a blessing as well as curse she thought. Nevertheless she would and could turn that to her advantage she determined.

"Show time!" she said to herself, as her keyed up healthy heart pounded out of rhythm with her seemingly leisurely stride, "now lets see which one of us is the cat or mouse?"

As usual just as if nothing was amiss she unlocked the door, J. J entered shouting, "It's just me Joanna, I'm home, my turn on the bottom bunk. I'm bushed. Hey lazy bones, wake up and out!" she said to the doll as she pulled herself in locking the door before pulling off her shoes.

Going immediately into the back chamber she quickly wiped off her make-up with wet ones she'd taken to using in the curtained alcove. J.J scurried quickly into her everyday duds clipping on the braid. She returned to the front cabin closing off the bunk by zipping closed the curtain. Joanna sat in the driver's seat as she realistically stretched feigning a yawn, pulling down the mirror to tuck wisps of hair behind her ears. Pretending to have a conversation with her twin she mouthed words for the benefit of the possible onlooker who you never know may lip read?

Many tricks along with insights came easily to the mind of this movie buff.

From the corner of her eye she caught the flash of that red plaid again scurrying in-between two vans.

She remembered the parable her Dad had told her when situations got rough, hot or sticky. Which in Joanna's case, they often did. For having been an overactive tom boy in her childhood and a tendency towards being impulsive in her adulthood did seem to get her into trouble.

He would look her in the eye and say, "You're standing in the middle of a road girl, and a truck is coming head on towards you, now you now have three choices. One; you stay there getting creamed. Two; you step aside to let it go by. Or three; you step away then come back onto the road to finish business. Which ever you choose you have consequences. It's your choice, plus you've got to live as well as deal with what you choose!"

He would then hug her, pat her on the back to walk away letting her select her choice on her own. As he went throwing over his shoulder he would say, "Whatever you decide remember I'm there for ya."

The problem was however, he wasn't physically there anymore for her, neither was Mom, nor now Sara. No fault of theirs, just the truth was that she was indeed on her own. Oh how she still loved her Dad, but he was no longer on this earth to give her that hug, just like Ma and currently Sara.

Yet taking his advice once again she reached down grabbing her iron baseball bat; she had chosen her path.

Joanna mouthed the words, "going to do a tire check while I get some fresh air with Sol," as she proceeded to leash Solomon then get out. With her back turned towards the general position of the plaid shirt she answered herself in Sara's voice.

Sol sensing something was wrong obeyed his mistresses beckoning, leaving his fruit for later. Once out of the truck he marched stiffly, tail curved up ready for battle. He kept close to her side without his customary dallying.

Joanna chatted aimlessly with Sol, keeping up the sham of business as usual. She whacked the tires with enthusiasm letting the observer figure out for himself she was not a shrinking violet type. Also she was sending a clear message to the unwelcome onlooker; meaning he could and would get the same treatment as the tires free of charge if he tried to come too close!

Just then a big red Kenworth passing by stopped. The window rolled down to show a green haired person who beamed a hundred watt smile.

Leaning out his window one could see his big arm which ended with a huge fist. It was the Jolly Green Giant. He had earned his name both because of his six foot four size, on top of having dyed his hair green upon a dare. Jolly was tagged on because of his good nature in addition to of the canned veggie advertisements. Jolly was a bear of a man, but gentle as could be if you didn't get on the wrong side of him, and even then it took a lot.

Recognizing him she waved smiling, Sol swung from side to side looking up at everything waiting to see what came next.

"J.J.," he joyously called out, "want me to beat up the tires for ya?"

"No thanks Green Giant, but I could think of a few heads I'd love to see roll at the moment!" she laughed back as she almost shouted her reply over the roar of the mighty motors turning.

"Name em Babe, for you it's done free of charge, has someone been bothering you or giving you a hard time love?" He responded really concerned.

"Ya, except for now it seems o.k., hopefully the one concerned has got the message!" Joanna replied.

"J.J., I've gotta park this thing, talk to me on channel eighteen wheelers, o.k.!" he demanded, not shifting his rig into gear even though other trucks waited behind him. Once he got her answer in a yes headshake along with the thumbs up sign he then moved his rig, not before.

Joanna having watched him pull out turned towards her cab hauling herself with Sol up into it. She mouthed for observer's sake that it was just her with Sol to the doll simulating the sleeping Sara. She unleashed Sol who freed returned to his dish of fruit. Joanna switched on the C.B. as was told to do changing channels to eighteen.

She caught the Giants inquisitive voice saying, "You there honey?"

"Yep, she answered, I'm here," she said into the mouth piece.

"Want to talk about it on the C.B., outside together, or over a coffee?" He offered.

"Stop by and pick me up. We'll chat outside at one of the picnic tables near by, O.K.? Sara is fast asleep after her all day outing, Sol who missed her will be all right, and me, well I slept most of the day so . . ." she faded off.

"No problem will be there in a jiffy!" The giant stated, "Ho, Ho Ho.!" And he switched off.

A few minutes later he lightly tapped on her cab door. Joanna who had gone to get a sweater for the cool evenings after the day's heat answered his knock by quickly getting out then locking up. Once installed comfortably at a table the Giant began his interrogation.

He was concerned for he knew Joanna to be the cool as a cucumber type, hardly ever being flustered for or over nothing. He listened gravely as J. J. told her story of being followed this evening.

During their conversation they discovered to their mutual surprise, moreover delight; they both had a pick up early tomorrow morning at the same place. The Giant's was a half load so he would have to high tail it to the next pick up after. Joanna's was a full load with three drops on her way home over the Canadian border. They determined to leave together for the pick up while leaving Sara behind for her shower along with time for breakfast at the truck stop. Joanna would then backtrack to the truck stop to collect her twin on her way back home. In a crowded place Sara should be safe they concluded.

This settled Joanna now felt safe again. Especially since the Giant made her promise to leave her C.B. on all night at the appointed channel with a promise to holler to him if anything went wrong. This was comforting; plus she knew of the tales of how light a sleeper he was.

That coupled with the stories of how in the past a few times he had foiled pranksters or evil doers due to this trick gave her confidence. His presence a few trucks away was reassuring in this lonely world and strange land. Alone sure she would have gotten through it too. Save for it's always easier with a little help from a good friend in times of trouble or worry. She was grateful for this intervention.

Back beside her truck the gentleman Giant said good night giving a brotherly hug, stepping back as he waited for Joanna to be safely inside.

Joanna unlocking the door was greeted by a huffed hissing iguana still on his guard mode.

"Whoa back, little demon!" the giant chuckled, "alls well."

The hissing wary iguana jumped to mistress's shoulder anyway watching her back. Ready for a fight, this was his human!

"Sol!" she screeched, "Your nails!"

Solomon immediately lessened the pressure as he kept a set of distrustful eyes upon the visitor. Hearing them both laugh he relaxed, a bit any way, for if mistress cackled with him also, he might be o.k. So the reptilian watch dog let his guard down to ride his mistress possessively into the truck.

The Giant having reassured himself by watching her switch on the C.B. plus locking the door left knowing that all precautions were taken.

He waved on his way towards his own mastodon.

Hidden a few trucks away opposite to the Giants, the Brian look alike made a call upon his cell. He relayed the bit of information he had been able to gleam here and there from eves dropping upon their often too low conversation. He confirmed the fact that both the girls were here; stating he was pretty sure that she had seen him.

Brian in response to his cousin's report gave him the order to follow her tomorrow making sure she was on her way back. The voice on this end grudgingly agreed to obey after loosing the argument.

Chapter 12

FIRST VICTORY

IN THE EARLY morn J.J along with the Giant were in the line up waiting to exit the parking. Only a few trucks were between them. Many were leaving this morning; therefore the gatekeeper sure had plenty to do checking the tickets besides collecting the dues.

The truckers all had the same thing in mind, meaning to be there at opening hours or on time for their appointments. J.J. chatted with many in the line up, aiming as planned to switch channels once out of the gate to be one on one with the Giant. Till then they all chatted. Some joked, and even shared their gripes along with their few praises about the trucking i n d u s t r y. Others in words showed their love of trucks and the road.

The Giant was an American who ran only the states, she a Canadian who did both U.S.A. and Canada. They had met at a McDonalds a few years ago while parking their rigs, just as for many a trucker a bond of friendship was quickly formed. These bonds of friendship were as strong as family ties often. Time and space did not seem to exist for them in their special world here. In trucker's friendships even if you had not seen each other for a spell, well the conversation seemed to pick up just where it had left off. Time and timing so important to drivers was left out only on these occasions.

This was one thing Joanna had always appreciated, even more so now with the void her immediate family's demise had left.

"Long distance Owner Operator . . . and proud to be!" was written in silver clearly stating her belief stretched across her ample bosom upon a black T-Shirt.

At last out of the gate upon the highway they matched pace though there still were a few trucks between them along with a few early bird four wheelers. Actually what the truckers called terrorists meant really tourist to the drivers. They had earned that nickname's description due to their often loosing the notion they were on the road. All that trouble was due to their gawking around taking in the wonders instead of watching the road. This bad habit resulted in uneven speeds, as well as being in general a danger; hereby becoming a terror for the long haulers or big trucks.

Joanna led the way to the pick-up having once been to that location before in the past. The Giant easily keeping up followed while chatting continually to J.J. about one thing or another. After about half an hour into the run trucks in the line up started to drop out taking various exits leading to their destinations. Three quarters of the way just one red sports car was left between them.

Oddly that wee sports car doggedly trailed Joanna. He did not take the fast lane nor do his thing as most people did. Instead he stuck like a greased suppository to her trailer's bumper. This alerted J.J. as it did the Giant, to the potential fact that the stocker may be back. Unfortunately he stayed single mindedly in the blind spot of Joanna's big side view mirrors. Also to her dismay the Giant had reported that the windows were deeply tinted making it impossible for him to describe the person. Even when Joanna swerved to try to catch a glimpse it didn't work for the ass plug swerved too!

The Giant had stayed stern in his own road pattern having heard J.J's warning about what she was to try, as well as what to watch out for.

Watching the scene play out before him he made a decision. Radioing to J.J he told her what he planned to do stating what he needed her to do to make it happen.

J.J listened closely for it was all said in a sort of double talk in case listeners were active. She began to search for the perfect stretch of road she knew lay ahead in order to put the plan into action. Shortly after their planning the trap they were upon that sought after stretch of less traveled double lane road.

"Ten four Giant, for miles the weather is clear, think I'll put up the sail now!" she said to the mouth piece just before putting the pedal to the metal. This immediately changed the once sluggish stroll of the big dog to overdrive.

She held down steadily gaining speed, putting a distance between her and the stunned driver of the red sports car. With perfect timing the big green Kenworth also did a show of speed bursting, overtaking the suspicious car. Joanna with her Pete ate the black ribbon at high speed. Oh how she felt excited for she loved the feel of its power surrounding her.

Seeing the Giant was out she started to downshift to match the sports car speed. Scouting ahead she kept a vigilant eye for any sign of oncoming cars keeping the Giant up to date. The red car was now obliged to take the alley between the two mastodons, walled in by the metal beasts. He did not know the green truck was a friend of the supposedly two girls in the Pete.

The giant had put his flasher on forcing his opening to enter ahead of the sports car. The little car strongly held his position behind or beside J.J till he had no other choice then to back down behind the Giant. This was yet again another confirmation that this was definitely the stalker.

The Giant burst forth again coming window to window position with the red sports car. Its owner then made a major mistake; he rolled down his window giving the Giant the verb sign that did not say you were number one. This certainly didn't put the Giant in a jolly mood, but it did give him a good look at the driver.

While keeping his own identity concealed by the glare of the sun he said to J.J, "The whale will now strike!"

The Giant when he had him placed just where he wanted him fishtailed it as the trailer bumper swatted the annoying road bug. The little car spun out of control. It crossed the shallow ditch to sink to its axels in the wet soft sand just by a fence holding in a herd of cows who booed the intruder. The Giant looked forward to giving J.J the blow by blow of this whales catch at their pick-up. For now he simply stated, "The fish is now out of the pond!" to J.J watching her gear down to normal speed.

She laughed back saying, "My knight in shinning armor. This damsel in distress thanks you for this victory. The next exit is ours Giant, we have got to share this experience!" which was more than a promise for in a few minutes face to face they did.

Solomon had all through this sat completely on the seat almost wishing he too could wear a seatbelt. He had soon gotten down from his perch sensing the static in the air just before the Pete burst into warp drive. Presently it slowed down again allowing the wary iguana to scramble once again to his perch. He was wondering if he still was on earth. He was, except he could plainly see mistress sure had a far off pleased look on her face. Maybe she had found the piece of cheese he'd lost last night he thought, while Joanna thought victory is best served warm in the hot sands of CA.

Chapter 13

FAILED TRAILING

JOANNA HAD THE time of her life sharing with the Giant the thrill of their escapade, laughing almost continuously about the stalker who looked like a cornstalk standing in sandy mud like sewage knee deep.

They joked about Solomon's reactions to the more than usual speed along with the less smooth ride. Together they fantasized. They hoped for a few scorpions or snakes to put the cherry on top of the cake scaring him as he had hoped to scare Joanna. May well be they probably would never know, however what they did made them strut almost as well as Solomon for the moment.

The Giant was able to give a facial description of the stalker confirming to Joanna it was the Brian look-alike. The news did put her out a bit. Nevertheless at the same time it proved she was really getting to the creep of a brother in law. His panic button could well be stuck with all she had seen as well as found out the other day.

The Giant once again rode off to his next pick up after making Joanna promise if there was trouble to give him a call on the cell. He knew a lot of truckers on the road. Just as he was sure many would step in to give a little help to a friend in need. Plus he had already called the Bulldog. He drove a beige Mack, The Giant told him to watch out for Joanna, keeping a distance for the first leg of her journey. Then afterwards, if need be the Giant would make other arrangements.

J.J feeling cared for, protected and safe had given the Giant a big thank you hug. He also got a friendly kiss good bye on each cheek to Solomon's dismay. The indignant iguana had watched from the dash of the truck, scratching at the window to no avail. Frustrated he took to vigorously pace the dash's length with his beards blown full out, tail up impressing many who saw him.

"She was his Human, Hands and tongue off her!" he had hissed, completely ignored by the two of them as his tongue snaked in and out!

Needless to say, Sol, after that rode Joanna's shoulder even if after awhile it became visibly uncomfortable for her. Nevertheless he persistently, over possessively hung on. The lizard kicked up a fuss when she tried to remove him. He was especially miffed when she got out at the truck stop again feigning the pick up of the awaiting Sara.

Nope, he decided where you go my lady I go, and that he did for the most part of the day.

Not far into the first leg of her journey a rasping Louisiana accented voice called over the C.B. with lots of static inquiring, "Are you J.J the Giants damsel?

"Sure am, are you the Bulldog, in a big Mack, I don't see ya," she replied still trying to spot him in her mirrors or ahead.

"Honey, I'm your invisible guardian angle, you see I'm a wee bit ahead of you but a few of my friends on the other channel were talking about a lady driver and the doll beside her in a big O Pete," he replied to her inquiry.

"What do you mean doll?" she asked back worried.

"The babe beside you in the passenger seat, the one with short hair, seemingly the guys you passed said you were twins or something, wow two sexy ladies under my wing!" Bull dog bragged back.

Joanna was quite relieved when she heard his explanation as to the use of the word doll! She answered back laughing, while reminding him that the Giant had first victory on him, and was waiting for her news tonight. She had played the CD with Sara's laugh joined in to make it all stick.

They chatted back and forth for about three hours more sealing the bond of yet another friendship born. They trailed each other chatting all the way with the voice of Sara jumping in here and there. It was carried on right up till where the Bulldog had to turn off for his drop.

It was then that Joanna finally got a glimpse of him; for he had slowed to almost a stop upon the shoulder. He too was a big man sporting a deeply creased smiling face. He stretched out waving goodbye to her as she came up closer to pass him by. Bulldog blew her and the doll a few kisses from his big beige Mack as they neared.

Over the C.B he laughed saying, "See now why it is not just because I drive a Mack my name is Bulldog. I have the shape, form and face to match the truck, ha-ha. Bulldog is my handle, and it fits me fine. You two girls are truly twin beauties, thanks for making the ride fun, over n out, put, put rrrrr" he feigned growling.

Seeing his amused face now confirmed all he had said as she along with the Sara doll had happily wished him a safe trip zipping by at a not too fast nor to slow speed. They had energetically waved back as they past to the good hearted guardian angle of the last four hours. Wholeheartedly thanking him for his time as well as babysitting.

There had been no sign of the Brian look alike stalker. Sol accompanied Joanna having a safe journey home. Compared to the first half it was an uneventful return trip. Solomon at last had relaxed after a day of sticking like glue to her, allowing her to once again drive the truck without his looking over her shoulder all the time.

As for the Giant, he had kept checking up on her each evening right up till she had her first night home. It felt good to have some one care about her without bad intentions. Joanna on those evening calls had even chatted with Poucette (little thumb), The Giant's French wife also from Canada, filling her in on some of the changes in Montreal since she had last visited. As big as the Giant was his wife was small, four foot eleven, she didn't hit the big five foot she was told. However they were happily in love with each other. Proof of that love was five healthy kids to their credit. Yep, Poucette had traded in the maple leaf for the star spangled banner for the man she loved, even gave up trucking herself. Something Joanna was beginning to appreciate more than she had ever before. Dang, must be that biological clock kicking in she told her self. That often became her justification, especially when she caught herself daydreaming about that hunk Gregory Armstrong, or of homes or kids running wild having fun while raising cane.

What she didn't know was that Calvin, once rudely swatted off the road, along with put in his place with the other desert beasts, had called Brian on the spot. Full of apologies he told his cousin what had happened. This had of course infuriated the dear fellow to the point of having hired a person to stake out the transport company he knew J.J. worked for. He was waiting for a chance to get back, or even and then some with his wife as well as her rough shod sister. If ever he could trace them or catch them on the road again. What he hadn't figured on was that J.J. had left the trailer at another point of business to be filled once again to hit the trail. She had posted the official papers giving her no reason to show at the Transport Company, depot or garage. Destiny so far was definitely on Joanna's side, or was it justice?

The hired man every day for a week had staked the transport company with no luck at all. Not one sighting, neither of the much sought after Pete or the twins. This of course had cost a pretty penny, putting a dent in the already low funds of Brian. The fruitless trying to trail her had failed, plus he did not have the cash he had hoped for by committing murder. All this was forcing him to back down some.

Brian was becoming one very desperate man. Totally bitter, nearly broke, plus mightily frustrated by the fact according to his belief the twins were the cause of all his woes; he became even meaner. The heartless money grubber deduced that it could not come to be that he had endured that family for nothing, time is money! And his time has got to be paid one way or another!

To date his investments had only got him the fringe benefits of a married man to a beautiful rich wife who was smart to boot. She had had the brains to continue to enrich herself as well as the power to dispose of her earnings. Brian had tagged along waiting or begging, sometimes earning handouts . . . feeding off as well as sharing her limelight. In reality the black heart was a well trained rattler waiting to mortally strike for self appropriation. Thing is, he had missed this time it seems. The snake oil slimed away brooding.

Chapter 14

THE MEETING

THE CALENDAR HAD changed months. December rolled in with howling winds, complete with an avalanche of that white fluff Solomon was not fond of. From his outpost, Solomon viewed the outside world which had turned even a brighter white today. He noted that yellow orange truck picked up small humans as it slowly went along. Seeing that most people were bundled up so that you could catch a glimpse of eyes only told him it was freezing cold out there. This iguana would be using the litter box much more frequently he now decided. Mistress would be carrying him more often, as he would get to ride under her coat or in her hood now. At least there were some advantages to that white fluff he thought as he absent mindedly scratched himself making the last piece of shedding skin fall.

Sol's shedding now complete he was once again the handsome reptile he was meant to be. He felt all male, and oh so good. Sol hated it when he changed skins. Each time he looked into that stand up floor to ceiling river he looked horrible. The skin itched too; making his humor along with mood swings much more apparent. The egotistical little fellow climbed down to do just that, look into the stand up river again. Yes he confirmed to himself he looked good, must go show mistress. He be lined it for the bed climbing the overhanging blanket. Making sure not to go anywhere near mistresses' tummy in any manner, way or form this time. He went to her pillow. Cuddling her head he laid on her hair wiggling to get deeper into the black strands.

Joanna came out of her now light sleep, thinking great I will be plucking skin out of my hair again. Lying back with her eyes fighting to stay open, she relaxed a bit endeavoring to ease her self into the waking world. They had got in late last night, having left the Tisson's around ten, their bedtime hour. The three hour plus drive had been accompanied by the radio man promising a storm with high winds. Just as they had hit their street the snow had began to fall. That stuff was picture pretty for sure as well as very cold. She knew that her partner in crime, Solomon would be changing his ways. Such as stubbornly refusing to in any way set his clawed hands or feet on that stuff unless there was no other choice.

It had been a great week for her and Solomon; a true delight where Joanna was able to be all that time just her self. It was so restful without impersonating Sara. The Tisson's had spoiled them with home cooked meals, smiles and much needed hugs. Past tales were relived as she brought them up to date both on the twin's alleged activities. J.J. even gave a quick rundown on the financial part of the mill to reassure them all was well as Sara supposedly said to do.

Of course they had been disappointed Sara had not come. Other than that they seemingly accepted Joanna's explanation that she wanted to do some work in order to be ready to leave with her for the next ride. Like kids to whom Christmas had come early they had enjoyed the gifts the twins had selected for them both on the Florida and California haul.

Joanna had seen a few problems brought on with time and by the aging of the Tissons at the mill. Her first aim had righted one by buying a used lift to ease the process of loading or unloading the logs. The truck with the clam was often on the road making it necessary for Mr.

Tisson along with the workers to do this by hand. He was getting up in age so Joanna didn't want him to overdo it. She had pretended to place a call on her cell to Sara to confirm the buy, and then went ahead with the transaction. To continue the sham, J.J. packed up the paper work to deliver to Sara. Joanna felt good about her decision, especially once seeing the appreciation in her surrogate father's eyes.

The mill had as always been doing well with excellent profits, so this expense could be written up into the reports easily as with her other buys for the company. It was common ground, well understood that meals were always given to the workers, meaning both breakfast in addition to dinner. So you could say the kitchen was part of the mills needs for business reasons, a sort of homey cafeteria. The stove which had already been overhauled numerous times however, still worked only on two or three of the rounds, all depending upon its caprices. As for the refrigerator, it no longer froze food properly. This made daily trips to the store another chore for the hardworking elderly couple to do.

Joanna had taken off with the company truck, going for the twenty minute drive to the nearby town known as Marysville. There she tended to remedy these problems by buying a new stove, along with a refrigerator, plus a new dishwasher. The dishwasher would be a first for the homestead. However, one she figured would free up time, thus making life easier for the wonderful cook, Mrs. Tisson.

The lady in question, with tears of joy had beamed with pride, moreover her appreciation upon the new additions. Nobody was the least bit sad to see the old things carted off to the barn. Joanna had paid the bills putting everything in order as well as had helped to install the new appliances. She had made sure all worked properly.

To continue the ongoing tradition Joanna had added to the wall of family pictures. Her additions consisted of framed snapshots of her as Sara, as well as herself with Sol. The elderly couple who looked on as she hung them were as swollen with pride of the girls as any true parent could have been.

Sol did his part to keep them healthy by busily chasing him.

He gave them reasons to laugh at his ongoing antics. Sol even daily supplied them with ongoing reason to remark his activities, reactions to things or chat about them. Sol had as always enjoyed his enlarged play ground to the utmost running by up one stairway then down the other one.

Just as in the past the twins had done themselves. One day he had climbed the mill's rafters. The hard headed little fellow refused to come down till closing time before supper. He had laid watching or dozing while basking in the heat given off by the combustion of the sawdust in the fire box. That source of energy in turn built up the steam for the engine to sequentially make the mill's various saws as well as machinery function.

Time to quit George had made to leave the mill by which Sol had gently dropped to his shoulder acquiring his ride to the house. Clara, George and Sara were the only other humans he freely interacted with.

They were to him his part time humans.

At the end of the week however, there had been a sticky moment.

Dear foul mouthed Brian in a hostile mood had called demanding to speak to Sara if she were there. The Tissons telling the truth had said she was not there. He of course cussing said they were hiding her. The indignant Mr. Tisson had replied politely to Brian's accusations. He did however say that he didn't lie like some he knew. He went on to state clearly that he was not obliged in anyway to tolerate such talk from an ill mannered upstart just before hanging up on him with a loud clatter.

The stately elderly smiled and walked away to finish what he was doing.

J.J now had some explaining to do, not easy for she felt awful lying to the Tisson's who held onto her every word. She told them that Sara, and Brian, had had a very big falling out. Therefore Sara, had taken a room at a motel in Joanna's name, to do her work while keeping her identity as well as location a secret. The Tissons shook their head with knowing expressions asking no more questions. They just specified that if the girl needed help they were there for her, as well as her home anytime; but for now they understood the situation.

Joanna was pleased with the way Brian had been neatly put into his place. However, this incident did add a few more chores to her personal list. One was the buying a cell phone for the Tisson's use while getting a new company telephone number. Next she changed the house number listing to confidential as well as unlisted. George or Clara would now give the new numbers with discretion to their chosen friends, customers, business people and so on. The cell would be for when the twin's called or when they were not in the house. It also served for company business, as well as for their use when they traveled for security sake. The Tissons this way could ignore or not receive bothersome unwanted calls. Joanna even thought of and ordered new business cards.

On her new to do list next up for J.J. was a trip to a dog trainer she knew of to buy a set of pet com watchdogs. Her handed out reason for this buy was to regulate the problem of some wood that was doing a disappearing act. One could stay out doors while the other would be indoors, each taking turns; therefore there should be no problem of jealousy between the German Shepherds. These dogs would in her absence watch over these two important people for her. Clara and George were all the family she had left. Joanna intended to keep them with her as long as possible. She did not now in any way trust Brian.

Therefore precautions along with roadblocks she steadily put into place. All the while hopefully leaving the elderly couple their freedom, yet in her absence protecting them as much as she could.

The couple were enchanted with these well behaved trained dogs.

They began to immediately search for names. That whole evening how they had laughed having fun trying to find suitable names for the new members of their entourage. They ended up with Hansel for the male and Gretel for the female. Both names the dogs seemed to accept, so all were content.

Maybe Joanna had been over protective. Possibly overly cautious, but she had professionals in the next day to install an alarm system in the house, the mill plus the barn on top of it. She told the Tissons that this system covered firefighting services, ambulances along with police. They both then were given necklaces with electronic medallions that when needed were to be activated by touch in case of whatever came up. This would alert the service who firstly placed a call to the house itself to see if contact could be established to offer help. If not it would send help right away, however if they were there then they may call a designated friend if needed. If no answers were to take place or a stranger answered these calls, then the secret pin was asked. According to the system's protocols, help and safety factors were well considered, and action took place assuring the required help would be sent on the way. The couple at first didn't feel at ease with these new fangled things. Yet seeing the importance they held to Joanna, along with her serious worry, they promised to wear them. In reality they agreed, they were getting up in age, so this could be good they admitted.

Feeling she had taken care of most possibilities of danger where Clara and George were concerned she had kissed them goodbye hugging them hard till the next time they met. Sol had done his version of the same, cuddling into them with his head flicking his tongue alongside their soft weather beaten cheeks.

Leaving while promising to give Sara their love, plus talk her into visiting soon she had walked with George to her camper trailed by Gretel who had taken to him as Hansel had to Clara.

"Is old Betsy in shape George?" she had asked looking him in the eye, saying more with her look than her mouth did.

"Yep the barrels are clean plus I even shot the old sawed off shotgun at a pesky skunk a few weeks ago," he had reassured her, "I have no qualms using it on vermin!" he answered also looking her in the eyes, communicating all that was left unsaid.

"Good, vermin at times tend to show up due to the need to calm their particular hunger or to do trouble, natural to their kind," she had stated, "Nice to know they won't overrun the place!"

George had hugged her again whispering into her ear, "Its bad dear?"

"Yes very serious," she had replied, "Promise me to take care of your selves, o.k., and do not to hesitate if the time should come?"

"No problem, though I for certain in particular cases prefer to maim vermin for life than kill, letting nature take its natural course, or the next up fix their wagon!" he had said to Joanna's surprise, "Make him suffer for hurting our girl! She is really alright?" He questioned anxiously needing to be reassured.

"All taken into consideration, as well as is possible, Mom and Dad are with her and with God's help we'll get through this," Joanna had said taking her place behind the wheel as George closed the door.

A tear had welled in the old man's eye as he sniffled. J.J rolled down the window, for he knew the girl before him even better than she thought he did. That is what forced the truth out of her to him alone.

George had drawn a wavering breath saying, "From now on it's to you I talk little lady. But Clara will need news from Sara. Hear me, you be careful now, though I don't know all of it yet, I feel it in my bones that much is amiss!"

Joanna had done a double take by the insight of the old man, but remembering he was the one who could almost always tell them apart she was not in a way surprised. His reaction to it all in a way did however.

She was especially quite taken aback when George without ceremony handed her a brown paper bag through the window. He had gravely said it was Sara's Christmas present ahead of time. George winked, instructing Joanna to open it once she got outside of the village in a secure, and secluded spot, not before. For her to use it to clear the vermin without hesitating. He hoped she'd take into consideration his opinion about living and suffering, learning the hard way; thus remembering it!

Joanna had heaved a sigh, she no longer was completely alone in her endeavor. The strong, brave aging man who had always shared Joanna's opinion about Brian now shared her silent grief. Two sets of tear glazed eyes then had met, locked, sealing a bond of mutual vengeance against the talked about vermin.

George bent down for a last kiss upon his cheek as he said, "For now no questions asked, but one day young lady before I too go to see your Mom and Dad you had better let it all out, promise?"

"Yes, I promise; for now it's good to know you understand some at least, now sharing my quest in a way. Do keep Clara out of this ok?"

She had pleaded.

"No, not till its time will I share this with her!" he in turn promised as he waved goodbye one last time watching the camper with Joanna and Sol disappear.

All the way home Joanna had felt a warm glow grow in her chest.

The heavy burden she carried now was in a limited form shared; as well as her thirst for righting things. Just as her hunger for preserving the family, and what was theirs. Yep, war was mutually declared on trouble seeking vermin.

This had definitely been confirmed when she had opened the brown paper bag as instructed by George upon the outskirts of the village.

Within she had found her own cleaned pistol. Included was a permit to carry a gun, along with her certificate of journalism. Upon her Dad's insistence she had trained to use the hand held gun, earning her permit to carry it. Thus fulfilling his wish while wiping away some of his worries. Mr. Miller had feared that his adventurous daughter would accept assignments in God forsaken places or situations. He had actually been relieved when his daughter chose to be a trucker in the end.

Looking to the nightstand she once again saw the black velvet case holding the gun. No two ways about it, George was far from being dense. Even her shoulder holster had been sent along, for when buying the whole kit and caboodle her Dad had left nothing out. Now George in turn had left nothing out. It was a comfort having it with her, yet s c a r y.

She wondered if she would hesitate to use it. Admonishing herself that though she could take a perverse pleasure in using it on Brian, she would only use it in self defense; thus in that case not hesitate. In heart she was not a killer. Except she did have a passionate conviction in taking a stand; be it verbally, or in dire times with more drastic measures for life sustaining reasons. She had a sense of morality, believed in what was right, sacred, her faith, her family, her love for others, plus not being killed, abused or robbed. She enjoyed life, usually having a love for adventure. Therefore her love of life extended towards others.

However, self preservation was also one of her major strong points. That is after that of her family, loved ones, the children and so on. Self defense in other words was a thing she believed in big time. Yet she preferred peace and harmony above all.

Stretching as she always did signaled to Sol she was about to get up. He skittered to her shoulder to playfully nip her ear. Joanna in a lighthearted mood grabbed him pretending to wrestle down an alligator or croc. It had been ages since she had so played with him giving Sol great happiness along with hope that whatever was wrong would work out one day, that they could be normal again, that is their normal . . .

The ringy dingy thing rudely cut through their laughter and playful hissing. Always on alert for its sign of coming to life Sol readily attacked as usual while an amused Joanna watched on. The new cell phone's case was already beginning to show battle scars. The thing silenced once again the ever victorious Sol strut to get a swig of water feeling like a hero for silencing that leather skinned noisy critter. He did wonder . . . now was that thing a vermin also?

Joanna as on queue picked it up just before it began to tauntingly sing out. The iguana made for it again, but upon seeing his Mistress shaking her finger at him he knew that was one of the no no's. Attacking the critter while Mistress chatted with it was out of the question. One lesson he had learnt the hard way in the past. So he grudging left her to it. Solomon returned to his water dish. He climbed up his tree where he watched with envy oozing out of each pore.

It was Rick, her dispatcher calling to see if she was ready to brave the road again tomorrow after her self imposed holiday. She agreed after hearing the where to, how much as well as the when. After hanging up she dialed the Tisson's on the new cell telling Clara that she along with Sara were taking off to North Carolina.

George grabbed the phone from his wife telling Joanna to take care of Sara, finishing with, "You know what I mean by that dear!"

J.J. shook her head solemnly promising to do so as if he could see, however she did voice, "if the need comes up, I'll stand up to be counted!" saying her good bye on a more cheerful note she hung up.

At last swinging out of bed she got into gear making a hasty breakfast for both of them then showering. She had determined bringing Sol along for the shopping would slow her down, so she left him behind sulking in his tree.

Putting the last can into the basket at the supermarket, who do you think J.J came face to face with? It was Brian to her dismay, doing his shopping also. He slithered to her side wearing a sneer which rendered what could have been considered a handsome face repulsively ugly.

"Where is my wife Joanna? He growled low and dangerously into her left ear.

She felt contaminated by the evil which seemed to pour out from him, as he oozed with the slime of hatred. Joanna calmly answered back, her heart in reality doing double overtime, "Why? Where she wants to be of course! I'm not her keeper, just her sidekick Brian," she impatiently answered.

"Ya, Ya, sure little J.J." he said menacingly dwarfing her by his tall body builders frame, "She doesn't answer her personal cell, apart from the bills, and of course that fax confirming the huge deposit in her personal account I have no real peg on her. What are you two up too?"

He sniffed in addition to snorting like the pig he was before wiping his nose with his sleeve.

"Caught a cold Brian?" cooed Joanna innocently, "What have you been up to?" she in turn replied turning the conversation around admirably as she stretched to take a lettuce from the counter. This movement allowed her holster with the butt of the gun to become slightly visible. "Me I'm on a mission. As for Sara, well you probably know more than I the where she is at, or coming from with her decisions to not see, or speak to you!" J.J. in turn sniffed, but took a Kleenex. "I'm in a rush, and would hate to finish this conversation with a bang. Sol is waiting as well as my boyfriend for supper, so bye. Just think, once Sara has decided to show, I'm sure you will be one of the first to know what's on or not!" She said as she had finished paying for her things leaving him completely plugged, scowling ruthlessly at her reply.

Brian stood near the checkout counter with a full basket of food. He was trapped, both by spectators listening in on the purposely above normal level conversation on Joanna's part; as well as the necessity to pay for his supplies. Legally along with for appearances, he had to stay put, as well as shut up. Something this person did not do gracefully.

Joanna, composed, calm, cool as a cucumber walked away feeling his eyes bore into her back like hot knives as she left. This doubled her pleasure; firstly his being so put out, and at last he showed his open hostility. He could prove to be dangerous she decided. Therefore Joanna confirmed to her self that from now on she would be more vigilant in her actions as to personal safety. At least now the game would be played with the players true faces shown.

The two had definitely squared off. It had been a face off like two sparing roosters. Joanna was in her corner fighting for her family and beloved twin. Brian was in his corner, fighting for his lust for money, along with his so far ill fated dream.

The hoped for outcome as far as J.J. was concerned was that justice would finally be served. Especially according to her and George's idea of it. Lately to tell the truth; George's idea had taken on an even sweeter flavor, especially after this last meeting.

Chapter 15

ROAD KILL

It was nice to temporarily leave the snow behind as they hit warmer climates in Maryland. Off came the big winter coats, light weight jackets were now donned instead. Joanna did the quick change, except for keeping her studded drivers gloves on. Maybe merely either out of habit or just to rapidly rig the Sarah doll's life like movements.

Sol was uneasy sensing the cloud over Mistresses' head again.

He rode the Sara doll's shoulder forever on the lookout for anything strange. Solomon to boot knew that he was in the last stages of his three month aggressively. That time of life where mating calls rang in his little ears. His presently high keyed brain was beyond a doubt, aiding him to be ready to take charge indeed if called for, or not. His new skin's green was even more eye-catching than before, plus his new spikes had grown out some. He now measured near four foot long with a possible two and one half feet to grow. His collar had had to be let out, even his vest no longer closed. Yep, he thought, this iguana was one great specimen of a male; he would appreciate any female, as she him. Conceited little tyke now wasn't he? Mistress could well be proud of all eight pounds of him as he entered his fourth year of a possible twenty five plus.

Doing their thing the two companions rolled along the open highway heading towards their destiny once again. Both were wondering what it would hold, but both were unwaveringly certain they would face it head on with no backing out. The sham of pretending to be Sara or that she was with her had now become second nature, allowing her to concentrate on safety precautions more. When Joanna's mind was idle it would flit from Sara to the Tissons; even to that unforgettable police officer. A thought this jealous green lizard was best without knowing.

Up to now she had not spotted anything out of the usual or out of line. No vehicles seemed to follow her, nor had there been any stalkers to her knowledge. In this state on her way to Raleigh North Carolina she could roll seventy miles per hour, which was a lot more to her liking than the fifty five in California. The thrill of being King of the Hill sitting in the driver's seat of an eighteen wheeler as always made her blood sing. This was the world she loved, as did the iguana with his head thrust forward in anticipation balanced upon the Sara doll's shoulder. Both were high strung, taut as a bow strings, consumed with the devouring sensation that something was going to happen . . . and soon!

They were to drop their load of furniture for Hamiscon at the appointed three stores which contained bar stools, tables, bedroom sets, along with one pool table.

The dock foreman at the first store had been particularly taken with Sol. He, himself, also had an exotic pet. His was slightly bigger though, an almost full-grown alligator which Sol did well to keep out of the reach of.

Solomon did less strutting around that creature keeping himself either upon Joanna's shoulder or head; anywhere, way up high, and off the ground please.

This iguana had survival instincts even though he was in battle mood.

Pictures were taken of both Joanna with Sol on his leash and with the foreman with his Big Al on a leash. Penned upon the photo man had written: little brother and his lady. Before J.J left quite well pleased with the enjoyable time there for the next drop, the said foreman had proudly given her a digital copy of the photo. Needless to say it was gladly added to her growing collection.

Meeting so many good as well as interesting hard working people was yet another wonder to trucking. Friendships, as well as memories piled up as you saw, learnt, and grew in wisdom, experience, besides knowledge on this road called life.

The second drop was one of those places where you wished you had a pop trailer instead of a fifty three foot one. She had to navigate between impatient drivers who wouldn't let her line up to do her backing up into an alley to unload. So it took well more than one try to get it in. This made Joanna quite angry. Not far off the idiot of a shop owner, along with his workers, just watched pointing while girly giggling instead of stopping the traffic. Hell they must be from that arcade gang of male chauvinist macho mongrels who thought women should be kept tied to the sink or stove by the apron. Flying Figs she had no beef with male chefs or secretaries, why did they with women truck drivers? If you can do the job, you qualify was her opinion, no matter the job or sex of the person. Joanna had proved over and over she could and did qualify. At last the rig was positioned to be unloaded; the docks plate was installed for the unloading to be done.

She got out of her vehicle with Sol on her shoulder yet leashed to her wrist. Carrying her delivery papers she went to oversee the unloading, making sure the right things got taken out and no more. One thing for sure, she was in a slightly foul mood matching her lizard's frame of mind.

Therefore, lifting even a little finger to help move the merchandise was out of her way.

Just as the last few pieces were taken out with the lift the owner of the business came strolling towards her. He was wearing a very smug grin.

Needless to say J.J. did not wear a matching superficial expression.

"Had a bit of trouble getting in did you?" he bragged, "I wonder what the owner of your rig would say?" he smirked.

Sol hissed, scratching the air as he sensed the antagonistic atmosphere, while Joanna struck out verbally, "I can tell you exactly what she would say! She would look you straight in the eye." And she did just so, "telling you little man to go where the sun doesn't shine with the brain full of it to match! You are so narrow minded your mama should of reprogrammed you at birth or drowned you!" she hissed in unison with Sol, as she poked him in his fat chest. "I am the owner of this bought and paid for in full one hundred and fifty thousand dollar tractor van. I have had the pleasure of doing Canada along with forty two states in long hauls, plus the displeasure to announce to you that you are the biggest jerk I have yet met in the forty two states along with your pals! If you wanted a faster service all you had to do instead of giggling like a little girl was to of had been a man getting off your duff to stop the traffic!" J.J said to the man now at nose length from her, as Sol nipped the air. "Make my day, sign here, you have got your stock," she said shoving the stack of papers into his line of view.

Sign he did with shaking hand as his pals and workers looked on snickering now at him instead of her, "You have character little lady, I will give you that!" he replied respectfully, "I won't apologize for my actions, am just sorry I hit a wicked harpy that can only bat her wings or shriek!" he said trying to get back at her.

A spark of contempt lit her eye as she coolly replied, "I have no problem with being called wicked, but I do with being called a harpy that can only shriek and bat her wings!" she said stretching so her vest pulled out to show the holster advantaging her ample bosom both now evident. "I'm a lady who knows what she wants in life; just so happens trucking is at this moment one of them. I also want an apology from you!" she said as Sol punctuated the air by whipping his tail.

The now unsettled owner humbly bowed his head, as the onlookers cheered her, "Sorry, "he said as he towed the dust, "now move out . . . please." He spoke for the first time politely handing her the signed bills.

"With pleasure, interesting doing business with you. Oh, just another little piece of info, if you want to lodge a complaint please do feel free to do so. My dispatcher is a gay, who has no problems dealing with your type!" the onlookers Hoodooed loudly! "Stuff that into your shirt you stiff necked little person. Try respect the next time as a greeting to those who are doing you a service which is their job. Big news flash, Mr. Nobody's Hero, slavery with women just as breeding stock or house cleaners are well in the past. Those women that choose that way of life are also respectable because they love the one they are with. You, I can't imagine someone loving besides maybe your blind, deaf and dumb mama!" Joanna also in turn whipped at him as a parting punch. She then strut off with her sparring partner, Sol. Head held high, back straight as a ram rod, she went at a leisurely pace to the cab door. Once there, she turned to cheerfully wave to the stunned, slack jawed owner who had been properly cowed. "Have a nice day!" she said beaming a huge smile his way.

Pulling out of the alley was a lot easier, for a worker now stopped the traffic. He bowed in reverence as he waved goodbye. The men there that day had a lot to chit chat or laugh about while they worked at their boss's expense. Bet some there may have changed certain views concerning women as helpless, headless, shrinking violets. Their boss had chosen to hole up in his office to give them freedom to do so without his hearing their tittering shaming him even more. The tables had turned on him . . .

Onto the next stop the two went filled with self-righteousness. It took a few miles for the pair to cool down. What did help was relating the story to another friend she had met up with heading in the same direction on the highway. He went by the handle Jukebox due to his capacity to sing almost all the hits; which he often did on the C.B. The two had chatted swapping stories till he turned off. Soon into their exchange she was her self again, laughing about the situation breaking the tension in the cab. This had allowed a keyed up iguana to once again relax a bit. Good thing too since the material upon a particular doll's shoulder had been getting worked over time lately. Joanna realized this fact, planning to fix the problem at their next stop, a halt upon the way.

She had stopped to put the doll in the rear again for her next drop, changing the stuffed sister's T-shirt at the same time. Not only had the material gotten shredded by Sol's repeated abuse with his long sharp nails, but it was scruffy also. Sol, polite creature he was had been using it as a napkin she deduced.

Once again back on the road after having had their meal, a TV dinner for J.J. accompanied by fresh cut fruit with greens for Sol. Both were in a better state of mind, much more calmer then before. At present with their bellies filled they relaxed somewhat.

J.J. had sprayed Solomon with room temperature bottled water she carried with her for this purpose. He felt refreshed, full, well pleased all in all with himself and his Mistress. He loved it when Mistress hissed in accord with him as he loved hearing her cackle. He felt as one even more so with his human as he installed himself with satisfaction once again as they pulled out of the halt.

J.J did her progressive shifting getting the rig up into cruising speed once more, shifting and changing up to the third level then with a flick of her thumb plus a quick push on the fuel pedal she gracefully with perfect timing slid into overdrive. She knew her rig loving the power it gave her. It was a 460 but had a 520 output on the drive thanks to her having had it opened once the guarantee was over. Another factor was her rig was not at a locked output, she controlled it rather than it controlling her. Thinking back to her last stop she figured she had driven that owner like she drove her truck. Hard yet controlled, with knowledge of what she had in her hands. Usually she wasn't hard on the machinery, but hard on herself; a sort of perfectionist to a point she expected a lot from her self. Joanna did her mileage as well as any other. She kept her rig's upkeep both in doing the maintenance as well as covering the road. This lady looked for no hand outs, but knew when to be humble, as she knew when to stand up. Yes, she well understood the differences made when found on either end of the stick. Sometimes it came to the simply saying, "Hit or be hit!" Do, or pay up. There were times to administer out tasks, just as at other times you did them yourself. So if a specialist was needed, that was it. If it was too big for her, out of her league, help was then found. However, she sure tried to do the most possible on her own.

The next stop, she was thankful to say the shop owner was a different breed then the last. He was a jovial fellow, an owner of a big multicolored parrot which rode his shoulder. This speaking bird clearly as well as quite openly spoke with a language as colorful as he was.

Sol upon J.J's shoulder did square off a bit with the parrot named Regan. To tell the tale; after Sol whipped him Reagan retaliated nipping back. They both seemed to then take their places. Barely tolerating each other that is, once their mutual testing of each other's finer points was done. Needless to say the two owners made sure not to stand shoulder to shoulder after that. Regan did however have the upper hand with his verbal capacities. He gave quite an impressive show of name calling to Solomon who did not take kindly to the outbreak. The lizard hissed back menacingly, beards standing and mouth snapping. It turned out both were in their aggressive stage the owners decided, kidding about their respective pets characters.

Trying to get the last dig Sol had jumped to the parrots perch.

Stretching out he lay now in the parrot's territory. Joanna had tied his leash to the stand assuming the wee lad wanted to be there, after receiving permission from the shop owner. Just then however to her surprise Regan took Sol's perch, meaning her shoulder. Nothing enticed him to leave her shoulder, treats, or kind words, even trying to pick him up.

He put on a show refusing to return to his master, squawking, "Help, rape, rape, help!" when the said person tried to retain his wayward pet.

What could one do but laugh at the jealous ways of these two sulking pets.

They definitely had a want to be winner temperament!

The shop owner comprehending their game quickly went to Sol offering him one of Regan's fresh cut pieces of fruit. Sol grabbed it with relish.

Of course that was too much for Regan. The indignant parrot returned to his master's shoulder without any more fuss, stating, "Not fair, not fair, foul play, Watergate!" loudly for all to hear.

The parrot's human had quickly stepped back so Joanna could retrieve her smug reclining pet; which she did. They both winked at each other as J.J. turned towards the dock's activities surveying the emptying of her trailer. She swept it out, to then go have her bills signed while the two pets eyed each other once again from their respective shoulders.

Joanna said good bye to yet another and as she turned, Reagan said his parting farewells: "Get a move on land lover, swab that #@!%* deck, hoist the !!#%**@# sail and get the @#!*# to it, auk awk, all hands on deck, storm ahead!"

Chuckling, Joanna did just that. Well her version of it, waving as she set out with Sol tightly hanging onto her headrest as he hissed back through the open window. That night both fell into a well deserved sleep at the truck stop parked between two humming reefers.

The next morning Sol was awakened by the ringy dingy mentally obliging him to start the day as he had finished the last, locked in a battle. This iguana was not missing exercise for sure. Joanna swung out of the bunk knowing full well it must be Rick calling to give her her pick up. Feeling the need to hit the trail back home, she had rushed, however not beating Solomon to it. She waited for the ever going ritual to take its course, allowing the wee lad to do his thing. Once the phone stopped, as usual it was time for Sol to back off so she could grab it. It had been established that for her pet to back off the cell phone attack it had to ring at least ten to twelve times. Other than that he seemed to wait for it to come back to life while still straddling it.

It was Rick. After checking the general where and what out she listened to the stated price of how much her payment would be. She accepted the load, a luxury owner/operators had compared to company drivers. J.J. installed herself comfortably on the bunk with pad and pen.

She listened while jotting down; the time of appointed pickup, name of the business, state, the address of, along with the telephone number.

Next Joanna noted the contacts name, description of load as well as the designated destinations, preferred reefer temperature, as well as opening times plus the days of business. Finishing up with noting the time of expected deliveries, with the name of the Broker for the custom clearances as well as his coordination's along with the preferred border exit. Then Rick gave her the route instructions. The designated farm was half an hour's drive off the highway on secondary roads, plus another half hour on a country road tucked in by a mountain in Virginia.

Every thing noted she proceeded to give a rendering of her three drops yesterday. That of course had Rick split in two laughing on the other end.

Once he had himself under control he asked, "How did you know I was gay?"

Joanna simply replied, "I lost two hundred and fifty bucks betting I could get you to look down my shirt before I figured it out!"

Bursting into laughter again, he gaffed, "It's got to be G.I.Joe, The Man, or Little Cowboy who set you up. They take me out bowling every once in awhile with their wives when they are missing a player. They always said I was a goldmine, to never change. Now I understand why at last!"

"Ya, sure thing, at how many others expense?" she growled playfully into the phone. "It's not my style but your choice of life my friend." Joanna said thinking of the cash she had lost.

Rick understanding at last how his fellow workers had been using him said, "I figure about every new driver went through it one way or another, come to think of it. One driver had even come in wearing just a G string swimsuit with a long shirt. I scolded him of course, saying indecent exposure was not one of our companies' policies. This is all really funny, what a gang of wise guys! Try not to feel put out J.J., harmless fun. If it helps, remember here you were treated with equality by being put through the mill. If bozo calls to complain, I will meet him head on. We can live without his kind. Up and at em girl, let me know when you have your load on board, bye." he said as he hung up quickly to answer the other phone which his assistant had been telling him was still on hold.

In a good mood, having got that off her chest she began to prepare her pet for the next part of her journey. Sol enjoying the attentive care was also soon in a better disposition.

Beautiful landscapes Virginia, Mountain Mama, but some businesses were way out. This was one of them. According to her instructions she was about twenty minutes upon this deserted gravel road from her pick up. That's when she saw him! He stood before a beat up car to the side of the road with its hood up waving her down.

The stranger came to stand in the middle of her half of the road. As she neared him she distinguished the long shape of a gun barrel lifting to take aim at the Sara doll. Without thinking it out J.J. automatically halted her downshifting to accelerating instead. Seeing this wild way of playing chicken forced the hit man to move over or be hit.

He managed to get off one shot only at the speeding on coming swerving metal beast with the iguana lady at its helm. The shot was poorly aimed thanks to Joanna's rapid thinking coupled with her quick reactions. It just put out her right mirror light shattering the mirror itself. He turned hurriedly trying to get out of the truck's way, but managed to get knocked over anyway. Joanna hearing the low sickening bang began to slow down figuring he would not be in to good a shape to do much harm if still alive. "Oh Lord, now what a mess, but self defense it surely was!"

Having stopped her rig, she got out into a cloud of bellowing dust. It swirled thickly; both from the spitting achoom of the air brakes along with the fact her eighteen wheels had just come to an abrupt stop upon the sun dried gravel road. Joanna advanced warily alongside her trailer, not thinking of the door she'd left open in her haste. Solomon had noted it though. Sol, unleashed crawled out to follow his mistress. Joanna inched to the sight where her aggressor lay. She now crept towards him, noting the gun lay ten feet away from him. She figured at least she no longer had any reason for the moment to fear being shot by it.

She toed the unmoving heap of human flesh. The Brian look alike, suddenly rose, grabbing her leg. Eyes opened wide, he sneered while cursing her with a harsh rasping breath. Sol assisting his Mistress whipped the offending set of hands resting on his human!

Straddling the assailants arm, he whipped with all his strength. The man's death grip suddenly became slack, freeing Joanna who had been violently struggling to get away. Realizing his Mistress was free, Sol jumped down to her side, taking a stance declaring his territory.

The man in question eyes suddenly glazed over then rolled up with just the whites showing. An expression of "what" seemed to freeze on his face as a dribble of blood ran down the side of his mouth. Before the drop of blood had fallen to his chest he had fallen back dead!

Later, Joanna, lying on her bunk, remembered how earlier that afternoon she had been shaken to the core as she had stared at the dead man. "Flying figs and goose squat! What am I suppose to do now?" she had thought horrified. However, she was not at all sad to see that man dead after trying to rekill Sara, and most likely her too.

Taking in the whole scene she had made a plan blessing the fact that empty fields surrounded her. Putting Solomon safely back into the truck J.J. at the same time had taken out a pair of well used work gloves she wore for maintenance or tanking. She had also gotten out her digital camera.

Joanna had photographed the man doing the job a crime specialist would have been proud of. She took pictures of him from various angles, pictures of her truck, the broken mirror, plus the rifle, along with the beat up car to the side. She even took photos of her brake marks. Finally she had taken a wide angle picture enclosing the whole scene, car, body, rifle, with her standing still truck. That accomplished she had went to hastily investigate the old car parked to the side.

Having returned to the functioning humming refrigerated trailer cooling for the load she was to pickup, she opened the doors. Grunting she had pulled out a roll of plastic she usually used to spread on the trailer's floor before loading messy products. Once on the ground she had kick rolled it to the desired spot.

Joanna had waited another five minutes more since having last checked the dead man. Still there had not been a pulse or any signs of breathing. She then had proceeded to literally bag him. "In for a penny, in for a pound." her Ma's voice had seemed to say climbing its way out of reprised past memories.

The survivor then went to re-investigate the old car. She quickly put down the hood. J.J next grabbed the keys on her way by to open the trunk to inspect it. The thing was totally empty, barren of luggage, or anything, not even a spare she had mocked.

J.J. had fought the dead weight landing her stiffening fish into the waiting trunk. Having sent his rifle in after him, she had swung the trunk closed.

After that she went to check out the contents of the glove compartment. There Joanna had learnt by the registration papers that this vehicle belonged to a certain Calvin Thorpe. He had the home address of California! More than coincidence she had deciphered.

Remarking the date upon a receipt she discovered he had bought the car that very same day from a gas station she had noticed in the last village she had passed. She had pocketed these continuing to examine the contents with gloved hands.

About half way through the remaining contents she had came upon about a dimes worth of marijuana in a plastic bag with a hash pipe. These she had left in the compartment. J.J, had however, taken the key with the big number thirteen written on a wooden tag. Of course figuring it out as being the motel room he had rented with the motel stub along with a pack of matches to confirm this. Since the matches clearly proclaimed its name, including location, she knew where he had holed up. About to get out after having rolled up the windows she noticed the ashtray was overflowing. He must have been waiting for awhile; this too she had photographed.

"What the heck!" she had thought as she had begun to check out another theory that would confirm this had been a well planned affair.

She had depressed the clutch, putting the shifter in neutral turning the key to see if it started. It immediately had sputtered into life squealing in pain from a loose fan strap probably. J.J. had then checked what gear she was in before letting go the clutch from habit for safety. It was then she saw the cell on the floor. Turning off the vehicle she had picked up the cell punching into the menu bringing up last calls received. Brian's number had shown clearly as the last three calls. Her blood had chilled by a few degrees. Yet J.J.'s determination to get him back became a hot coal that quickly erased the chill. Joanna had jotted down on a crumpled piece of paper she had found in her back pocket the names of 6 people she had discovered in the repertoire along with their numbers. She had decided she would leave the cell hidden under the seat after taking a photo of Brian's number displayed.

Getting out of the vehicle she had locked up while looking at the cardboard sign she had left saying, "Back in a flash, to get my trash!"

Grinning she had pocketed the newly acquired set of keys plus other information give aways she'd found while leaving the canned road kill in the abandoned car, "Dead skunk in the middle of the road," she sang as she got into her truck returning to her usual duties. Her hands shook less but her tummy was upset.

Back on the road looking back at the event she said out loud to herself, "I'm beginning to be a real cold, Bitch!" disgusted with the latest events.

Now parked in a safe place totally exhausted she dozed off to recuperate a bit.

Chapter 16

COLD MEAT

JOANNA WAS RUDELY awakened from her fitful sleep due to an annoying crack in the hastily closed curtains. This opening allowed bright rays of first morning light to pierce the rear darkness.

Her ongoing thoughts picked up where her mind had let off to sleep.

It had been hard to not let on how upset she had been once at the well equipped organized farm. The folks here had greeted her by kindly, inviting her to join in to share their outdoor meal. Their big point was that she would have had to of waited on them anyway whilst they ate. So she had on a tipsy turvey tummy added ingredients to her heaping served plate. Not making a very big dent in it she had excused herself after jokingly stating that she could drive like any man, but still had to put up with women's biological problems. Then she hurriedly disappeared around the barn's farthest corner to barf.

After such a show they had not insisted upon her finishing her plate.

They did though tend to keep a few feet from her, just in case. Once the van was loaded, once again ready to leave they deemed it alright to approach her; since she had not disappeared to throw up again. The kind owner approached to give her her papers. He had asked if she felt well enough to leave, or if she had need of any assistance in any way.

Joanna had once again found herself in a position of having to reassure people she was alright. A bad habit of late she would love to break. Once again she had sung her song that sleep was a must, then all would be well again. The owner had told her she could park her van to the left in the huge yard to take a snooze for as long as she wanted too. That is exactly what she had done after calling Rick to say she was loaded.

Now fully awake she hauled herself out of the bed waking Sol with her movements. She dressed hastily, fed Solomon while munching on a cracker herself as the truck turned over to bring up the air pressure. Joanna would have preferred to of had awakened in the dead of the night, but thank the Lord at least she was up early. She did a quick quiet checkup of the vehicle, verifying the reefer's fuel as well as temperature. Once back in she did her log book, filling out the vehicle inspection paper; marking in the broken mirror she intended to repair later on.

Joanna pulled out of the silent farm still in the throes of sleep.

Starting to backtrack to the highway she soon came upon the beat up old car parked at a standstill upon the side of the road. She slowed, coming to a full stop. Looked around the fields from her high position confirming to herself she was alone out there. That is, except for an iguana and a dead man.

Leaving Sol in the truck again she got out, put on her gloves again heading towards the trunk of the car which her trailer end was almost even with. She took out that set of keys, opened the trunk which did due to heat smell bad. All was as she had left it. A dead man bagged in a roll of plastic.

She could make out his vague form through the layers of thick dirty clear plastic. She stepped back a bit turning to open the reefer door, then grabbed the wrapped dead man which she hoisted with difficulty to her shoulder. She almost buckled under his weight. Winded and shaky Joanna took the few required steps to swing him off her shoulder to the high floor of the reefer. From the waist down he now dangled like a rag doll, and he was no friend of the Sara doll. J.J. struggled till she got him all in. She threw the gun in on top of him after taking out the bullets.

Sweat mixed with tears marred her face. Closing the reefer's doors she locked up putting on a padlock. After that she went once more to the car. This time she closed the trunk going to the driver's door. Joanna unlocked it grabbing the cell phone hid under the seat, she slipped it into a big baggie she had brought along for it. Locking up she scurried quickly to the truck, got in to start her engine, pulling out almost immediately.

Five miles later she met an old truck rattling along towards her full of workers sitting on home-made wooden benches. They all waved recognizing her. They cheerfully sang out good wishes for her trip home. Some were even shouting: name the baby after me, joking of course in reference to her vomiting. Yet she speculated, were they seriously thinking she was pregnant due to her excuse? Hells bells, in her head she had meant to insinuate her period. Joanna however waved back to the smiling faces wondering what they would do if they knew she had cold meat along with the veggies in the reefer?

A gentle short lived rain began to fall, erasing Joanna's tracks upon the road as it gathered force.

Chapter 17

ON THE BEEF OF DISCOVERY

Solomon watched the rolling scenery unfold as he and mistress ran the highway riding towards home. The Sara doll gently swayed as Sol every so often peeked into the newly replaced mirror watching what they left behind.

They had just crossed out of Pennsylvania into New York. J.J. had had just time enough to give a call to Daveda while in PA. and that did her good. Joanna needless to say respected all road regulations not wanting to get tangled up in any way with the law. She was nervous not wanting to draw attention onto herself hauling the side of beef she did not want discovered.

The Canadian border was getting closer and closer as miles sped by. J.J. knew she had to get rid of a certain carcass before going through customs; this of course was bothering her. Not being a practiced crime person and all she was sure she had made mistakes. Except for; hey she was doing her best to stay alive. J.J was working hard to keep up the sham, along with getting Brian to go over the edge without past killing her also. This was getting a bit tougher, which the events proved all too well. What more at the moment could a lady trucker do, besides keeping her business going while taking care of her pet?

Stopping at a tourist halt, she had bought a coffee after using the facalities at the halt. Sol since the snow preferred to be either carried or to stay in the truck. This time Joanna had left him in the truck. As she had looked over her shoulder while leaving she could see he was now on the dash doing his version of watch dog. Once in the building she looked over a batch of tourist brochures seeking answers or possibilities to her dilemma. In other words she was looking for a way out of being the one put behind bars for something she was not entirely responsible for. Though she believed in the death penalty for hideous crimes, she had not thought to be the one to deal out the decision or to make it happen. No use crying over spilt milk she decided, better to look for a solution.

Just then her eyes fell upon one brochure in particular, "Uswego, the city that harbors a few secrets . . . deep water ports . . . on Lake Ontario . . . 35 miles from Syracuse!"

"Bingo!" Yes here it was, she had thought, us we go to Uswego to give him the same burial rites as they had for Sara. It was on her way to the Alexandria bay custom border. What a relief! The side trip fit nicely into the allotted time she had left before her deliveries. Especially considering the fact she had not taken the day off given her, but had chosen to continue to do some mileage. The reason was simply to have as much space as possible between her and that abandoned car.

Yes, this could be perfect. That is, if she could pull it off. Truth was J.J didn't want to meet up with too many difficulties that could force her to change her plans.

"Destiny smile upon me. O Lord forgive me. I really didn't mean to kill him, it happened as I'm sure you seen. Now I have to deal with it. This to me is the only present solution taking everything into consideration," she said as a silent prayer. Joanna waited with eyes closed tightly for a moment. Nope, she was not hit by a bolt of lightening like in the comics.

Amen to that. With more confidence then when she had entered she left the building.

Joanna's step was lighter now that she knew where as well as how she was to go about the upcoming task. Back at the Pete she joined the small crowd of tourists taking pictures of Solomon hissing at them through the window while pacing. She listened to their comments along to what their guesses were as to what he was. Coming to her pets rescue she set them straight stating that this was not some alligator baby or croc. Sol was a vegetarian; his kind was known as Green Iguana's due to their skin color.

She explained he was now approximately four years old as well as roughly at least two feet under full growth. Once the usual oohs and ahs were said; she made way to she get into her truck. From there, she waved good bye to the onlookers as she pulled out. She now had a plan, a vision, plus a mission concerning the beef in the back. J.J. had taken to referring to him as such "the beef," for it seemed to disassociate him from human makings.

Making the getting rid of bad meat a lot easier.

Further along the way she had turned off into a closed halt parking in the back. Getting out, she left the frustrated iguana to once again pace the dash. The spot was empty, surrounded by bush. Just right for what she intended to do. Joanna went into the rear section after putting on her gloves grabbing three tough burlap bags from the mill she carried with her to put soiled or heavy things in. She used garbage bags for putting away garbage, plus lighter things such as dirty clothes or whatever. A supply of bags were always handy to a trucker. Then

Joanna took the cell phone she had turned off still in the baggie with gloved hands to stuffed it into her coat pocket.

Setting out to the edge of the asphalt she proceeded to put stones along with rocks into the bags. She lugged the one third filled bags to the back of her trailer, ready to continue her work with later on. Rotating around she returned to the front of the van. Joanna grabbed a roll of cord she had with her in the compartment under the bunk, along with a big flashlight.

Promptly she unlocked the padlock to heave in her bags of rocks chanting as she did so: "Baba black sheep, three bags full." As always her sense of wry humor showed up in tough situations. At this moment, here now, in these circumstances, she considered her self to be the lone black sheep.

Climbing up into the trailer she went firstly to check the produce she was carrying with the flash light she had brought along. She continued her inspection of the thermo kings contents. Now looking at the temperature recorder she confirmed to her self all was well. The doors being closed made it a grisly place, cold as hell in addition to pitch black with a dead man. She kept the light on.

Her chore taken care of she now got to work on the meat. Joanna worked busily unrolling him a bit to put in the rifle along with the bullets except one as proof if needed. She then added the cell which she had emptied of all calls, including numbers into the makeshift body bag. Joanna tied off the ends tightly with the cord, doing the same for the middle, making a neat package. She had left open loops at each tie line. Using her pocket knife she had cut the cord after assuring herself the knots were tight. Moving to her three weighted bags she readied them for fast tying into the loops with cord long enough to knot left hanging. The body was enough of weight to carry without the rocks for now.

She'd tie on the rocks just before dunking him. This done she figured it was only decent to at this moment give him his memorial service before sending him to his premeditated watery grave.

Still on her knees with the flash light upon the floor like a candle she began her slightly painfully twisted talk with the Maker: "Lord I didn't know him, and what I saw I didn't like. Just the same, maybe you knew of some good in him, even liked him for that. Truly sorry for the part I had in it, but as you know I acted upon self defense. I admit it's a lot easier to forgive him now, knowing he's dead and all, unable to continue to try and kill us again. I ask you to do whatever you think is best for his eternal place of existence. I accept your choice, though I don't think he was saved.

Nor maybe even believed in you very much; that is, seems so to me considering what he seemed to do for a living. But you're the boss and you know a lot more than I do. What's spiritual is now due to this accident in your hands, and getting rid of him, sadly in mine. Lets please try to work together, to make things right. I know vengeance is yours, so please feel free to do with me as your will. And forgive me for the pleasure I feel knowing he is dead. I intend to put his body to the water hoping he'll stay there as you know. But if I do get in a mess, grant please, that the pictures prove my and Sara's innocence. It's been a rough time lately, help it to go easier I ask, or get right again soon. I wish I could see Sara again but . . . well like I said; you already know that, one day I hope to be with her again.

Amen"

Getting up she felt better, ready to do what she was going to. She had done better by him than he would have done by her or Sara for sure. Locking the doors of the reefer once more she went to get back into the truck. Except for just as she turned the corner of her trailer she ran head on into a male's hard chest. Letting out a screech she backed up. Visibly shaken, flashlight raised in defense she stared wide eyed at the officer.

"Whoa little lady, didn't mean to startle you," he said shaking his head, "you alright? He questioned as she brought her ready to strike arm down.

"Yes," she breathed, "I was not expecting to run into somebody!" she kidded as her hand set upon her racing heart, "What is wrong officer?"

"Nothing, I was just checking that no one was doing dirty deeds to the building. Seeing your rig parked here, I came to check out what was going on," he said by way of justifying his presence.

"Oh I see!" she said, "as you can see I was not doing your described dirty deeds," she partialy lied? To lie or not to lie, a Shakespeare voice sang in her ears. "Just checking my cargo while making sure all was as I wanted it to be, ready to make the drop," she said telling the truth. "I was verifying the temperature recording device along with the placement of the cargo; roads are pretty rough this year."

"Oh ya, ain't that the truth! So all is well with both of us, but tell me what is that critter prancing on your dash?" he inquired genuinely curious.

"Solomon," she replied, relieved to see the change of subject as center of interest." Come, I'll introduce you!" which she did. After chatting for about fifteen minutes, while showing off her pet along with answering questions, the officer at last left.

It turned out that Officer Hamming was looking for a pet his daughter could have in an apartment that was hairless due to her allergies. After speaking with J.J. he now thought he would choose a lizard. Waving as he left he wished her a safe trouble free trip home. Joanna hoped his wish would come true.

Once again alone with Sol she wiped her brow saying to the little fellow, "Now that was close, real close, we were on the beef of discovery boy, and you saved the day! Mommy is so proud of you, come get a kiss along with a hug my hero," and so Sol did.

Evening had set in, hopefully that was good as she took her turn off to the beefs chosen resting place. It was Sunday so most folk were indoors after the weekend or resting up for work. In her present situation she considered that routine a great system which was very much to her liking. She made her rig crawl along a road that had a small yet hard shoulder, which dropped off suddenly to swiftly moving murky waters. Joanna was looking for just the right spot to do her hasty burial at sea.

A wee bit ahead Joanna could see what would become her chosen spot. It was upon a stretch just after a slight curb with a line of trees hosting no houses close by. This is it she thought to her self pulling the parking brakes donning the work gloves. She went rapidly to the rear of the truck. Before getting the body out Joanna took a good sized rock from the shoulder throwing it in over the edge. Listening to discern from the sound it made hitting the water she defined the approximate depth of the water by ear.

Good news, it was deep, which answered her needs. In a flash she was unlocking the trailer again. She climbed in. Being so close to the edge she had determined that she could tie on the bags of weight to the body while literally under the cover of her trailer. She hastily prepared doing just that.

Deciding there was no real good reason or logic in forcing like a bull to get the body out she rolled it to the edge of the trailer. Shoving she watched it fall with a sickening thud. Well he doesn't feel pain anymore she consoled herself, so what.

Jumping out, she noticed a set of car lights far off coming her way. She froze for a moment watching. The lights glad to say took a turn into a driveway about a quarter of a mile back.

"Lord this is sticky!' she breathed to her self, "Lord please, if you had wanted it otherwise you should have let me know before I got him out of the trailer!" she then got down on the ground to roll her piece of bad meat the few feet left to his resting place.

With a splash he hit the water to immediately begin to sink out of sight to J.J's relief. Dusting herself off she closed the reefer doors. Feeling free with one burden less, she ran to get into her tractor van. Around three miles further she turned her rig around in the empty yard of a fishing store closed for the evening.

Backtracking she was soon once again on the highway. Feeling much better about the approaching border, she promised herself once across the line they would park it for the remainder of the night. Yes, at the first opportunity they would rest. After all, they no longer had anything to beef about.

Chapter 18

RUNAWAY

FEELING REFRESHED AFTER their down time she now turned into one of the last truck stops on Ontario land before Quebec. They were both famished. Many others seemed to have the same symptoms, or either stopped for a break or who knows, maybe to just chew the rag this early morning. Some may of had slept there for the first parking by the main building was chock full. Joanna had to park way in the back of the second parking across the street. She had flawlessly lined up her rig and backed into one space blind side after adjusting her eclectic mirror to do so on the first shot. This got her the thumbs up sign from a few fellow drivers hoofing it to the building with pack sacs on their backs, most likely going for their morning showers. Joanna bumped up the idle after pulling the brake knob to set it to work. The specific achoooo as the air was released alerted a sleeping iguana that they had stopped.

Sol jumped to her lap after she had moved the big multi position steering wheel up allowing her space to get out of her seat. She cooed as she rubbed her pet telling him that yes he was to accompany her here. J.J. was a regular client stopping quite often on her numerous trips; well known, furthermore liked by the owner. Here she was allowed to bring Sol in for a meal.

As usual when she knew she was to make a pit stop she had done a quick halt on the shoulder of the road earlier to put the Sara doll ahead in the back. Not wanting any close encounters that would bring on trouble. Trouble she had enough of without chasing it she figured. J.J. now took all precautions possible, staying in public or traveled roads when possible, that is when she wasn't obliged to do a secret stunt or deed.

Her delivery time was after the dinner break, firstly at the Marcher Central, than as soon as possible at a few brand grocery stores. Noting it was only six thirty am, she rejoiced that she had ample time to eat, as well as dawdle. J.J. was so near to home she would take her shower there. As a quick fix Joanna had done her wash ritual in a microwave heated margarine dish of water this morning. Sprayed Sol then giving him water which she had doctored with vitamin and calcium drops to keep her pet healthy. She had not fed him nor ate herself, so this savvy iguana knew food was to be served indoors. Figuring out that they were at this particular stop the wise critter knew all to well the routine and he loved it.

Entering the bunk J.J. snatched a big snazzy well used golden rhinestone covered purse. She used this for her pet's transportation at this particular stop. The twins had bought it together at a flea market.

They had laughed at the flashy hideous thing, but having concluded to their knowledge of common friends as well as family it would and could only suit Sol. They bought it. Of course they did comment that only Liberachie, the piano player along with Solomon could love that thing. Solomon did love it; he climbed into it claiming it as his. He loved things that were shiny or sparkled. That was way back when he was a lot smaller, meaning when he fitted completely into it. Sol would back then poke his head out to take a gander at the world outside his flash house, but stay there contentedly for hours. Not long after the girls had used it to enter their reptilian pal into this particular truck stop on their way to Indiana.

At first when Sol poked his head out to get his food the owner did a double take coming quickly to their table thinking it was a snake.

Being reassured by seeing the four legs on the creature he took a liking to the little guy. Even from the start Sol had a character that would charm those who gave him a chance. Once receiving permission to openly enter, it had become a habit for Sol to eat there when opportunity allowed.

Seeing his flash house now got him all wound up as his hunger like a caged creature in his tummy was gnawing and twisting his innards. It was really his truck stop, plus oh joy, he was going to get a meal with service. As soon as his baby blanket was put in, Solomon eagerly crawled in unassisted. However, to his surprise now not only his tail hung out one end, but his head was also over hanging the other. Had Mistress washed and shrunk his flash house, or had he really gotten that big he wondered. No matter, he seemed to plead with Joanna. He smacked his lips signaling to her he was ready to go in addition to being very very hungry. Grabbing her coat along with the bag which Sol was in; she forgot to leash him before leaving. She cuddled the purse with her pet inside her loose parka, protecting him from the northern winds while sharing her body heat.

Once inside she met the owner by the cash out for the store stall.

He could be easily read as he looked at her free hand, head, then to her shoulder. He was searching for Sol. Bringing the wee lad into view still within his purse, the owner gaffed seeing the pompous iguana with head and tail sticking out. He reached for Sol; J.J. gave him up. Petting Sol, now on his shoulder the well pleased truck stop owner proceeded to lead them to a table. He signaled to a nearby unoccupied chatting waitress who hurriedly answered her Boss's call to serve them. The owner made it clear; V.I.P treatment, specifying Sol's order was on him.

Settled comfortably she ignored the stares from some customers who didn't yet know of her or Solomon, she read today's breakfast specials on the board.

She ordered a combo plate of two eggs, bacon, fried potatoes, beans, toast and a hot chocolate for herself. For Solomon she ordered a plate consisting of; two thin sliced cumbers, a few sprigs of parsley, celery tops, along with a few cold canned green beans, two stripes of fresh green peppers, one piece of cut up lettuce and a two thin slices of radish, topped with a small piece of cheese.

For desert here or on the road a cup of the house's fruit salad without the bananas. All that with Sol's special dish filled with fresh distilled water please. Joanna did not want an iguana with the runs due to having drunk strange water.

Sol sat patiently in his flash house waiting while the waitress well amused at Sol's order scurried off to fulfill it. He loved the attention he got. Looking over the many people in the restaurant while tasting the air he enjoyed the thrill of having so many things to excite his senses.

The waitress came back shortly pushing a high chair laughing at the questioning looks of some.

Joanna lifted Sol out with his baby blanket to install him in the chair; with his tail hanging out the back hole. The owner had a year ago cut out that hole to accommodate this particular client's needs in its wooden back. Solomon in gold had been painted across the back.

Joanna took the mini bib upon the table of the chair putting it on her excited pet.

That did it; those that had cameras began to click away at the comical sight of the bibbed arrogant iguana sitting in his baby chair. He sat in his kingly chair with his front hands on the table anxiously awaiting his plate. He loved to pose. One trucker fashioned a crude crown out of the silver paper from his cigarette pack setting it upon the wee king's head.

Another volley of snapshots was taken to stop only for the intervention of the waitress serving his and J.J.'s plates.

A star had been born, many watched avidly as the odd couple did their thing. Joanna cut up his food while he waited politely for that to be done before attacking it.

They ate accompanied by camera flashes every now and than. It felt good to be what she hoped safe for now, well surrounded by jovial people who weren't seeking to harm her, her family or her pet.

Having eaten her full Joanna lit one of her rare burn sticks. Sol forgiving her this lapse set into his dessert dish visibly enjoying himself.

He put on a show of being the perfect gentleman even though juice did dribble down his chin. Joanna like an absent minded mother out of habit dabbed his chin with a napkin as she read a newspaper.

Heinze strolled in joining their table bringing laughter along with conversation to the two. They chatted as he waited for his combo plate with of course a bottle of ketchup on the side. Sol continued to chomp his way through his dish of fruit.

Feeling good socializing with humans, Joanna noted her now full pet dozed contentedly. His head was leaning on his highchair table beside the empty bowl of salad. Now he innocently drew stares to his cute disposition, which sparked once again camera's to flash as they captured this sight.

Chatting aimlessly with Heinze they soon became caught up in a heated amicable discussion about politics. Fifteen minutes later, she did not see her unleashed pet climb down from his chair making for a certain lady. The person was wearing a woolen cap with a big pair of oval sunglasses. She had been silently sitting alone looking on while drinking a hot chocolate. The oversized coat gave no definition of her form. Only the delicate nose gave the impression of female, for even the chin was partially wrapped in a scarf she had not let down to drink with her woolen gloves.

The stranger did see the pet coming towards her, without fear she greeted him with a friendly rub on his head. Than she seemed put out all of sudden. Not knowing what to do, she called the waitress at the next table asking her to tell the owner her pet was here. Seeing the waitress continued to finish taking the order before doing so the impatient mystery person got hastily up. She headed for the exit almost racing the waitress in the aisle. Sol stunned by the volatile reaction sat gloomily on the abandoned table looking as if his best friend had let him down.

Even before the waitress managed to get to her table, J.J. had felt an "Oh no!" come as a warning to her thoughts, feeling all worried all of a sudden. It was quite well justified, especially after noting Sol's disappearance. The waitress confirmed her troubled thoughts as well as her sudden need to be concerned.

Joanna got up quickly to retrieve her pet looking to see where the mystery person was to apologize to them. As she turned from side to side a whiff of Quelque fleurs perfume, French for some flowers, came to her nose. Immediately recognizing that smell as having been Sara's favorite, J.J. associated it with the lady in the next stall. That person also wore a woolen cap along with sunglasses. However, that lady in question denied being the one who had sent the message via the waitress.

Joanna looked up just in time to catch a glimpse of a similar person paying at the cash. She hurried back to her table plunking Sol on it with a quick "Watch him for me a minute; will ya please," to the confused Heinze.

She turned to just catch yet another peek of the person exiting the door.

Grabbing her coat she proceeded to run after her. Out on the gallery she surveyed the parking area. J.J. searched as she looked for the mystery person among the trucks, or on the road crossing to the next lot. Just then, J.J saw a blue Rabbit made by Volks Wagon. It was in poor condition, but it was with the same lady at the wheel pulling out.

Joanna wildly signaled to the person hoping that she would stop. The strange, yet seemingly familiar person just waved while continuing to pull out totally ignoring Joanna's clear invitation to come back. J.J. noted a dirty Quebec license plate, except she couldn't make out the numbers on the rapidly departing vehicle.

"It couldn't be!" she said out loud to herself, "It just couldn't be!" she re confirmed sadly.

Besides, Sara wouldn't be caught dead in a Rabbit let alone one in such poor condition. Her sister had always preferred flashy sports car that were far from falling apart! Ridiculing her self for such false hopes, she returned to the restaurant, dismayed it wasn't true. Now she was the one who wore the look of her pet; both stunned by the reaction in addition to the overly hasty departure. They both could not understand the whole scene. Yet they both felt abandoned as if they'd been let down somehow.

Back in the restaurant the high chair had been whisked away, the changed atmosphere seemed calm but curious. Some were even possibly confused as she was by the whole thing. Joanna though knew for her part she had just given chase to an innocent mystery person.

Probably scaring the daylights out of her too boot for heaven's sake.

"Shame on you!" She admonished herself. "Wishful thinking could get you in trouble, especially with the game you are playing yourself.

Think, just maybe that person was another setup by Brian," she concluded to herself.

Heinze still at the table sat there with empty arms. Worried once again she asked him where Sol was. He then just pointed to the flash house that had seemed to of even lost most of its glitter. In the purse one could easily make out Sol nestled there. His head was no longer stuck out as before ecclesiastically looking for action. Only his tell tale tail could be seen hanging dejectedly more out than in. Solomon, wanting to be bodily out of sight in his depressed state had done his best to hide. Compassion for her forlorn pet welled in her chest as she held back tears for both of them.

"Odd," Heinze sadly said, "he just crawled in all by himself and didn't come back out, she didn't hurt him did she?" he anxiously inquired.

"No," Joanna replied with a tired sad smile, "it was just a case of mistaken identity. He is feeling bad about it as I do. I think Sol is right though, time to go," she said patting Heinze on the back thanking him as she wished him well. Picking up her downcast Sol still hiding in his bag, she turned to the general crowd saying, "good bye all, safe trip."

Accompanied by a chorus of good wishes to her retreating back she made to leave at a much slower pace than earlier. She paid her bill, left a tip, hugging her pet within her coat to return to the truck.

The warm interior of the cab greeted their wind chilled bodies.

Pleased that she had left it turning with the heat on she sat for a moment in silence; as a big single tear welled, overflowing to slid down her left cheek.

Sol had wriggled out of his purse still hugged by his mistress.

Sensing her need for love he climbed to her shoulder. There Solomon cuddled her as best he could, putting her need for comfort before his own. Touched Joanna caressed her pet giving him a peck on his cheek in return.

"We are one odd couple Sol," she declared as she put her pet from her shoulder to the empty passenger seat to shrug out of her coat, "You know for a moment, just a moment there, I really thought maybe it was her, just maybe it was?" she faded off. Sol seemed to shake his head in agreement. "Whoever it was, why did they runaway, why the rush? She had seemed almost scared, as if she had been caught doing something.

It isn't a crime to drink a coffee or coco! No, it certainly was not a sin. just like it wasn't an offense to pet you!" Joanna thought aloud.

Getting behind the wheel again she checked her gages making ready to pull out. J.J. had not installed the Sara doll. Joanna just didn't have the heart now to look into its empty glass eyes again wishing those eyes would sparkle back laughing with or at her. To feel Sara's clothes under her hands or smell that perfume would definitely open the flood gates she was fighting to keep under control. Heck she scolded herself, here we have a person that could get rid of a piece of bad meat and she blubbers over a stranger who runs away. You are weird Joanna, she told herself, defiantly on the wild and wacky side.

Back on the highway her thoughts kept turning back to the scene again and again. Even the fussy iguana had felt an invisible bond or was drawn to that person. What in heaven's name had got into both of them, what made the lady a runaway? She questioned once again on automatic pilot heading for her drops. One thing for sure, it was not only weird as the rest of her life was lately, but all three of them she was sure seemed to wear new emotional scars. Telling her self enough is enough, time to get her fuddled mind back on her job, she came to this deduction. All three had been confused, plus shaken not knowing why, acting as well as reacting on instinct, except maybe for the runaway?

Her thoughts now more centered on what she had to do she drove on. That is apart from the invading fact that all day her mind had procrastinated as she watched out for a battered blue Rabbit. Now was it either for confirmation or understanding. The riddle however, stayed unsolved. Yes, into the cold ravaged wind swept scenery the little blue Rabbit runaway had disappeared; leaving a big hole that Sol along with Joanna couldn't understand as to the why, nor the who. Adding it to her list of questions to be answered once she too was on the other side of heaven's gates she buried the past as best she could once more. It helped while it worked, staying below the surface and not to deep to constantly prick the heart. It was the only way to survive the pain and loss in order to continue on with journey, her quest as well as her life. The runaway was no longer before her but behind her.

At this very moment she along with Sol struggled forward and onwards.

Chapter 19

I SPY

AT LAST THE downtrodden weary travelers arrived home. They both felt none too soon as J.J. let the pack sac slide to the floor along with the bag of dirty clothes in her hand. Joanna moaned a sigh of relief. Locking the door behind her she went straight to the bedroom.

Sol was let loose on the floor allowing him to run freely. He too had one idea, so he headed to take care of business. Something both had been holding on for awhile now not wanting to stop unnecessarily. This taken care of, she put him in his tree, then undressed to fall into bed.

Quite the contrary to her usual way of doing things, yet the need for rest overpowered the needs of good habits.

"To Hell with it all!" she said to herself, "tomorrow I'll finish unloading and clean up, I'm bushed!" J.J slipped into a bothered sleep.

In her dream she chased mystery ladies again with Sol, as the dead man gurgled with laughter at her from his watery grave while of course Brian urged him on to continue tormenting her. It was not an easy sleep for her or the iguana that now lay besides her making running motions as he too ran in his dreams. Their horror along with their confusion had followed them even on that journey, to the land where things should have been peaceful and sweet.

A man dressed in black surveyed the truck he had followed from the company garage. He watched the apartment's lights as they winked off.

With satisfaction he noted the address down on a piece of paper before leaving to also go to bed. He started the blue sports car driving off as silently as he had come, making plans. He too had many unanswered questions. However, his dreams of late were also filled with horrors; except they were horrors which he joyfully inflicted.

Blankets knotted around her combined with her dreams had her awaken during the night stifling a scream. Switching on the lamp thankful it was not Calvin's hand once again upon her leg, she drew a deep breath to calm herself. Her sweat soaked hair clung in damp tendrils to her neck and head while beads of perspiration now dried upon her brow.

Disgusted with her present state, not having showered before going to bed, she got up to do something about it. Glancing at the illuminated face of the clock she saw it was just three thirty in the morning. Though still fatigued she reckoned she would be unable to revert to sleep dirty as she felt. With lagging step she went to do once more what had to be done for the moment rather than what she really felt like doing. Though it was that decision that made her take a shower rather than sleep, the warm soapy water felt good as it washed away the sweat along with the grime of crime. She had just finished shampooing, beginning to rinse her hair when she saw Sol. He was scratching, silently pleading with her, seeking permission as well as help to join in the cleansing process. Joanna lifted her pet over the edge. He looked as if he needed to be revitalized by the water also. Both stood absorbing the warmth, feeling as if the water washed away more than what was visible to the eye. Cleansing together the dreams of past events in a silent solemn shared ritual; the shower continued to run over them for another ten minutes. Feeling once again alive instead of half dead she at last climbed out of the shower refreshed, feeling clean. She let Sol continue to soak for today he was not playing in the rain room as usual. While he had his time she dried herself off. J.J. blow dried her hair enjoying the normal activity now feeling calmer. After brushing her teeth she turned off the shower to give her loyal pet, that partner and true friend, a well deserved rub down.

Sol showed his appreciation by rubbing his cheek against hers flicking his tongue to taste her fresh skin in a lizard kiss. Once upon the floor he followed his beloved Mistress to the open small kitchen com front room. There he climbed the easy chair to stretch out on its high back to maintain a look out. Sol was still worried over J.J. Their lives had become weirdly stressful; though neither understood nor knew truly why. All this lizard could do was just deal with things as they came along, like a pro up at bat. He, Solomon, was and would be there for his human anytime.

Joanna began to fix herself some toast, not forgetting a plate of veggies for Sol. The kettle hissed as it began to boil, a sound Sol always associated with a battle cry. This seemed to flick a switch inside the wee fellow where he became suddenly alive, truly well on red alert. His eyes no longer drooped just as his tail became less slack. This iguana was once again ready to go. However no danger showed even after he checked the place out. Therefore he devoured his meal with gusto forever on the watch just incase. He had not shown an appetite since breakfast the day before, but now he was starving.

There had not been any switches flicked in J.J.'s body so she munched her toast which felt good settling in her empty stomach. Sipping her hot chocolate she came to the conclusion she was returning to bed once having cleaned up after their snack. Worn out she knew her four legged pal would be disappointed with her need for sleep. Yet she was exhausted after all she had been through.

The kitchen cleaned she got out a tattered cat ball giving it to Sol.

That should help him spend some of that extra energy. She on the other hand went to acquire energy flat on her back. It didn't take long for her to slip into a more restful sleep. Her pet wrestled his ball chasing it all over the wee apartment.

Feeling at last recharged she awoke around dinner time. Sol, for the last half hour had been eying her from the pillow. He was mentally trying to convince her to wake up. He had grown tired of playing with his ball, and now that the toilet paper had been pulled all over in addition to shredded, that too was also boring. He had even helped Mistress by partially emptying the dirty clothes bag, now won't she be happy?

Joanna swung out of bed feeling much more human along with more her self to go potty. Of course on the way she was greeted by signs of Sol's activities all over during her down time.

"Sol, bad iguana, bad, bad bad, how many times did I tell you not to play with the toilet paper?" She asked shaking her finger at the iguana in question. She paused as if waiting for an answer which of course didn't verbally come. "Do you realize that was the last roll you rascal?" she said picking up the less shredded pieces to take with her to the toilet, "Bad Iguana, BAD BOY, Ooooh so bad!"

Sol hearing her water fall decided to slink under the sofa for awhile.

That is till Mistress was in a better mood, maybe his helping with the clothes as he had done will please her he contemplated. Nope turned out it didn't, so he stayed there falling asleep himself quite tired after having been so helpful.

Joanna picked up toilet paper saving the good pieces for in case till she got to the store. She picked up the dirty clothes Sol had left all over. Then she picked up the pack sac to unpack what was still clean.

After that she went to pick up the tangled bed covers in order to make the bed. At this time she was ready to empty the truck doing the usual preparations for the next time out. Meaning Joanna picked up the last ride's mess.

The washer was doing overtime since Joanna had decided to wash the bunk bed blankets as well as the bed clothes, the dirty clothes along with the towels. The dryer clinked as a snap of her black pants hit the metal cylinder while it made its whirly sound along with the sloshing of the washer. Her equipment was not the modern silent ones. They had been bought at a used store just in case she did not like apartment life. Humbug, their music did not bother her if it got the job done. Housecleaning, even washing she could meticulously do well.

It was cooking she totally botched.

As Evening came around after checking her reserves of salvaged folded toilet paper she decided she didn't feel like going out that day.

Calling up an order of hot chicken for herself plus a specified fresh salad for Sol she sat to smoke one of her cigarettes while waiting for it to be delivered. The small apartments along with the truck were now both sparkling clean, ready for whatever. Pleased with her accomplishments she smoked. Sol once again forgiven had climbed Mistress's jean clad leg to her lap to take pleasure in being petted by her; even if it was absentmindedly.

Soon after smoking she got up again switching on the television, settling into the easy chair with Solomon stretched out on its head.

Listening to the news she had began to doze off, however, hearing the name Calvin Thorpe she was once again wide awake.

The newscast spoke of the abandoned car being found day before yesterday with nothing to show to who the owner was except for the license plate for a lead.

Joanna ticked off, mistake number one in an imperfect deed in her mind.

The news lady now said they had tracked down where it had been bought earlier that week from a garage who had given a description of the buyer that matched the name of Calvin Thorpe, reported missing by his father.

"O.k." she thought to her self, "I should have blown up the garage man, and the license bureau, as well as sabotaged the computer systems!" she ticked off mistake number two, a, b, and c in errors to the perfect unwanted but mixed into crime out loud to Sol.

"Mr. Connor Thorpe, well known in the metal industry, as well as a wealthy land owner, was said to be quite worried about his son's sudden disappearance!" belted out the news cast man.

"Mistake number three," she thought, "now that goes way back, should never of tangled with that Thorpe family!" but the name Connor Thorpe was added to her list of possible dangerous people.

The newscast continued, "It was also discovered by questioning people in the same village that Mr. Calvin Thorpe had rented a room at the village hotel, but after two nights stay did not return."

"Oops!" Joanna said getting up off the chair going to the pile of pants yet to wash, "mistake number four to five. Should of burned down the hotel, possibly knocked off the owner; why not the whole village in a Rambo stunt? Plus I should get rid of these papers along with the keys," she said out loud. She dug them out of the pockets with ungloved hands. "Swift Joanna!' she said to herself realizing that error.

Returning to the front room she looked on again as the news cast person said, "Further investigations were being made by the newly promoted inspector Gregory Armstrong of California, along with the authorities of Virginia. We will inform you as the investigation proceeds of new developments. If you have any information please come forward."

Joanna stepped backwards looking at the incriminating evidence in her hands, "Number six I shouldn't of been seen by him, much less moon about him!" she groaned. "Hopefully Sol and I will be lucky seven and not get caught!"

Swiftly going to the back door of the wee apartment she unlocked it. This gave her access to the rest of the cellar, a storage cupboard you could say. The furnace room and another entrance to the basement was also part of her territory if needed. She went to the wood and electric combined furnace glad to see it had recently been lit by the upstairs people and now was burning ardently. She threw in the papers. After taking the key chain off the wooden plaque she threw the plaque in too.

Joanna checked the other entrance door making sure it was well locked doing the same for the basement windows. Returning to her apartment she relocked the door behind her putting a chair upended with the back under the knob. This she didn't understand why but felt better it having been done. Drawing closed all the blinds also made her feel safer. The key still in her hand she silently planned to throw it into the lake next chance she had.

Joanna was scrubbing her hands when the doorbell made her guiltily jump. Drying them she went quickly to see if it was the delivery man or the police. She breathed easier seeing the bagged order the young smiling male face showed her through the door window. Allowing him to enter she paid for her meals, tipped him saying thank you as she followed him out locking that top stair door too. Going back down the stairs she re entered her small haven locking that door behind her as well.

Turning she looked at Sol who had positioned himself anticipating her next actions in front of his empty food plate. J.J. laughed at her pet as well as her self as she said to him, "Who needs police to be locked up, we don't now do we Sol? We can do it ourselves," She declared accompanied by the continuing newscast droning in the background talking sports.

They ate in compatible silence, both lost in reflection. Sol day dreaming of the happy times they had had recently in the big litter box state, while Joanna pondered about the discovered uncorrectable mistakes.

The meal eaten, a quick cleanup done, Joanna went to put the last batch of wash to wash; which comprised of the offending jeans she had emptied the pockets of earlier. Adding extra soap along with a spot of Javel water to the filling tub, she dumped them in, feeling better about the fact traces were to be wiped away in the wash. Wouldn't it be nice if memory could be so easily dealt with she reflected?

Snatching up the bundle of clean bed clothes from the dryer top she went to make the bed. Making the bed made her become conscious of how tired she was again. Undressing she noticed the bedroom blind had still not been drawn. She closed it going to turn out the lights on the other side.

Once in bed she turned out the lamp, but switched it on again to go turn on the night light in the electrical plugging. Solomon followed her to bed falling asleep cuddled to her with her small soft work calloused hand lightly upon his back.

Meanwhile out in the street, having watched the blinds being drawn along with the lights go out, he once again started the motor of his car to drive off. He was disappointed that she had not gone out that day.

As the blue sports car slipped away into the night a black Chevy pulled out to follow at a safe distance.

Watching the two vehicles drive off a bag lady scurried into an old beat up blue Rabbit to follow the black Chevy also at a safe distance.

Joanna along with Sol slept oblivious to all this, lost in their uneasy respective dreams. Joanna felt watched as she dreamed of cars driving off into the night, following who knows who.

Chapter 20

CONFRONTATION

THE NEXT MORNING after having chatted with George and Clara, Joanna felt better; even though she spoke to Clara as Sara as George had asked. While with George, straight as herself, as promised. She didn't enlighten them of any details pertaining to her last trip, nor her walk on the wild side.

She had reported simply saying it had been an interesting trip.

Joanna did however thank George for his gift saying it had been handy though not used. He caught the drift not asking any questions. Ringing off just after George's anxious, "you have gotta visit soon to fill me in with the details, meanwhile do take care of Sara as well as yourself!"

That call did her wonders making her feel cared for as well as loved.

Seeing her meager supply of salvaged toilet paper diminish to one sheet after her morning absolutions she felt obliged to go to the grocers as soon as possible. Therefore, after getting ready to do so, once dressed she called Sol to leash him. Joanna had made a resolution, not to return to the same store where she had met Brian last time at. So it was the mall, as her self, for it also had a Metro.

The two now set off in her camper. They gracefully slipped into the flowing traffic. Joanna was not aware of the car that followed her but a scant three cars away. Glad to be on the road again, Sol vigilantly surveyed the surrounding vehicles. However, being now at eye level with some of them he menaced the drivers who came alongside. Sol took a stance, staring down at the shorter stock, letting them know that he saw them. Hissing he declared his territory, as well as his Mistress' being off bounds. Joanna laughed telling her pet that she had heard of drivers with road rage; but never of four legged passengers with road rage. This was undoubtedly new to her, definitely a first!

Concentrating on the oncoming Montreal Friday traffic plus being now in the second lane, J.J did not see whom her pet had seen. A blue Rabbit came along side rolling all it could to pass as peeling paint caught the wind.

Sol recognizing the runaway excitedly whipped the seat, however, in those close quarters J.J. got the tail end.

"Hey, watch it," she yelled vexed at her pet, "what has gotten into you?" She asked looking over his way to just catch the sight of the blue car turning off into another lane. "Damn! Sorry boy, I missed her, thanks. I ask though, could it be less painful you're getting my attention next time? You're a good watchdog!" she said putting on the flasher to change lanes as she slowed down not to miss the exit.

It also just happened to be her exit to get to the mall that the runaway rabbit had taken. Just maybe their paths would cross she thought hopefully. Who was that lady, plus for God's sake why did she seem so damn familiar to both her and Sol yet work so hard to be a stranger?

Exiting she drove the few hundred feet to the mall, then turned into its huge parking lot, "No sign of the Rabbit, it must have found a hole somewhere Sol!" she said. While keeping a watchful eye for a free parking space, she also surveyed the lot looking for the blue Rabbit.

"Well she did it again Sol, disappeared into thin air!" She stated just as she spotted a car leaving a space near the entrance. This she quickly advanced to claim. "Well we have our hole Sol, let's do it. "She backed her camper into the space. A tight fit since the parking spaces are now made smaller; taking more into consideration little cars than what she considered a real vehicle. "We're in, now let's get out," she said grabbing her pet as she got out locking the doors.

Once in the mall she dallied here and there with Sol on a leash to the joy of many onlookers. While Joanna was standing at a store window, openly admiring a certain top and pants set there came a well dressed man who cleared his throat trying to get her attention. He kept a safe distance from the strange green creature.

"Madame, Madame please!" he pleaded for her attention.

"Please what? She asked back, except in reality J.J. had pretty well figured out what was up.

"Nothing, Madame," as he drew breath to continue.

Joanna cut in before he could say more, "If nothing why are you bothering me completely destroying my day out?" she replied vexed.

"Sorry!" the confused shopping center manager stated, now abashed by the attention they were getting. He once more drew a breath before continuing his endeavor to get her audience.

J.J. like a shark smelling blood cut in again, "Liar, if you really were sorry you would leave me alone!" She squeaked indignantly as Sol jumped to her leg hugging it comically looking like a child seeking protection.

"Madame it's my job!" he replied truly exasperated now.

"You mean this shopping center hires dirty old men to harass young women?" Joanna asked feigning she was horrified. She reached for her pet like a mother for her child, hugging Sol to his delight.

"The sign says no animals," he tried once again to convey his message.

"Pray tell what you are doing here Mr. Pig! I'll say from experience accosting young women innocently passing the day while bringing cash money to your establishment. The sign says no dogs, look it's a dog barred off in that little red circle sir, this is not a dog!" She replied still clutching her pet.

The man in question had been the last few minutes a soft pink. But then understanding the sense of her answer being deeper than mere words his shade soon began to change to a darker tone. Beyond a doubt the poor man was beginning to loose it. Steam seemed to be coming out of his tightly buttoned collar under his tie. His face was turning a beat red from the heat which rose now to his forehead. The crowd watched.

Joanna watched. Sol watched. All were waiting to see what he was going to do or say next.

"That . . . means . . . no . . . an . . . i . . . mals!" He forced from a smiling red face between clenched teeth.

"Oh, that's all, no problem!" Joanna said ecstatically smiling or was it smirking as she petted Sol's head returning to view the window. She once more ignored the poor man to his anguish. J.J. had all of sudden felt highly amused, elated in fact with an irresistible urge to giggle. Odd she even felt proud of her self. This was fun!

"So!" The man who now looked like an extinct dodo bird waving his useless arms on either side of him stated as he tended to bounce upon one foot.

Quite a feat as well as quite a sight one must say. Joanna really had to bite down hard on her lip not to crack, "Oh I figured you meant that!" she responded boo hawing the air as she pawed it with her free hand then clicking her tongue while rolling up her eyes. She shook her head negatively. The crown enthralled by it all giggled encouraging J.J to give him another round, and she did by saying, "Solomon is not an animal!" she enlightened him with childlike innocence.

"What do you mean he is not an animal?" he growled with impatience letting his frustration take toll; "He has four legs doesn't he?" the man in huge volumes, along with high decimals; number eight on a level of ten spoke; or screeched should we say, drawing an even bigger crowd.

Children begin to cry because of this hollering man. Mother's comforted them while giving him the evil eye.

"Why sir, Solomon is a reptile!" J.J. once again enlightened him, with her big eyes opened wide, "can't you tell, so not being a dog like circled in red along with not being an animal the red circled dog means, he has every right to be here. Even more than you or me who are animals or mammals who are considered an animal!" Joanna explained to him.

"I mean anything that is not human is not allowed in the shopping center! He corrected himself, now extremely aggravated to the crowds delight.

Joanna loving the show couldn't resist going all nine yards to get another dig in, "Liar!" she called him another time, but she smirked openly.

"Lady, why the hell am I lying this time?" the frustrated manager screeched as if Joanna had his tubes in a knot.

"This center has major stores right? She paused as he shook his head yes, "Also a few pet shops?" she finished.

"SO!" he balled looking down at her with his head cocked to one side as his arms were winging up then down.

"The living creatures sold there are not humans; they are animals, reptiles, birds and even fish! Plus, they are all for sale right?" Joanna asked looking up at him one hand on hip insolently.

"SO!" he repeated along with the same weird body language.

"If you weren't a liar you would have realized that!" she replied defiantly.

The crowd howled now in chorus when the poor man grabbed his ears while saying, "O.k., no non humans allowed in the shopping center, that are not for sale!" The manager realized his mistake. As well as how his troublesome choice of words invited hell on earth from this irritating woman at his side. Yes this woman who used his own words as weapons against him. Thus he quickly corrected his phrase, "for sale by the pet shops or stores that is!"

"Liar!" Joanna yet again replied to this tormented man in the throes of public humiliation.

"WHY AM I A LIAR NOW MISSES KNOW IT ALL!" he bellowed making Sol hiss to which J.J. coo ed reassuringly to her little one.

"Non humans who are on sale in the stores or shops are allowed right? She looked him in the eye waiting for confirmation.

"Yes, so?" he confirmed as he repeated his little dance to the crowds j o y.

It must be a nervous tick Joanna decided before explaining her reasoning "Tell me Scotty, do we just beam them out when we buy them or is there some obscure underground tunnel we must use?"

J.J. counteracted his song and dance as the onlookers beamed their pleasure.

"Ok lady, non humans are allowed only if for sale in the shops or stores plus those bought have permission to pass through on their immediate departure after the transaction! The manager said all in one breath, now doubled in two, hands on knees looking up at her from the loud exertion, "and I am not lying!" he tacked on, "Please take your reptile out of this center, you are bothering the shoppers."

Exercise at its top Joanna surmised amused, he had fenced it in pretty good too, but not good enough, "Am I or Solomon bothering you?" she turned asking the crowd beseechingly while cuddling Solomon batting her lids.

"No!" they roared back with various comments like we love it, keep it up, and so on.

She turned to the manager," another lie see . . . ."

The manager knowing he had lost the battle decided not to lose the war, "He stood straight, loosened his tie, smoothed his hair, to say, "finish your day, but please don't bring him back!" than he walked away all dignified. Rather stiff like someone who had had an embarrassing accident to tell the truth.

"The crowd cheered then began to applaud Joanna who curtsied as she waved turning to once again view her window. She had at last decided to go buy those clothes. The manager, well he broke into a run to the finish line which was the sanctuary of his office. The last of the crowd dispersed after taking a few more pictures. Joanna with Sol entered the shop. They were serviced with reverence.

Presuming this was Sol's last visit to this mall, at least till a new manager took over; Joanna took him to visit the pet shops. Word had traveled fast, at the speed of sound. She was greeted with gusto. Sol got the royal tours as J.J. tagged along enjoying it all. At the first shop the owner noticed the wee lads vest was tight, soon to endanger his armpits by shafting. He remedied that by giving him a new one in a sparkly gold material. J.J. bought vitamins along with calcium drops from that shop.

The second shop not to be outdone took thirty percent off her purchase of a bigger carrying case to replace the old flash house.

"Isn't this fun?" Joanna asked her pet as they strolled towards the Metro. Both had not noticed Brian following. He was walking at a swift pace trying to catch up to them.

As she turned the corner, he cut her off leaning against the wall as if nothing was amiss. "Nice show a while ago, I enjoyed it! Hello my beautiful wife look a like sister in law, how are you as well as my beloved? Where is she, just as pray tell where is Calvin?" he sneered. "I advise you not to make a scene!"

"You quit the show Brian, you know a lot more than I do about what is going on, or where they are, so why don't you tell me what is up!" She sneered back. "Remember we are in a public place and only you will draw attention if I begin to scream as you run away."

Sol sensing that this was not fun for his Mistress hissed as he whipped this man he detested so. This action forced Brian to back off out of striking distance stifling a yelp.

"See, proof you don't want to draw attention, now do you Brian to your uncouth ways?" She taunted without disguise.

"Later Joanna!" he promised; "When you don't have your public!"

He said as a confirmation to his threat. Then Brian stalked off with his hands in his fancy black jacket on his way to Sara's and his blue sports c a r.

A bit shaken but pleased she had stood up to him J.J. continued to the Metro. The promised threat given in the confrontation chilled her.

Yet, Joanna knew his downfall was rage, while her strength was her love for her family. She courageously continued on, now knowing danger would be lurking at every turn, dark alley, or mistake she made.

Chapter 21

FINAL COMBAT

JOANNA PUT THE last bag of groceries into the van. The male of the two hung from the head rest surveying the pick up. Joanna in turn scrutinized all other humans passing by within eyesight.

"One thing Sol, you know having hit bad patches more often than not lately, you learn to appreciate the good times!" J.J. conversed with her silent pet. "Hey, weren't we at our best with that manager?" she asked him continuing as if he answered. "Even when old Brian there slithered into the day we held up. Many thanks for the piece of tail boy, your timing was perfect!" she looked up at her admiring pet as he seemed to mouth his ascension by snapping the air.

At that moment she had finished loading the many bags. However, she double checked making sure she had not forgotten the toilet paper.

Nope it was there, so all was well, so far anyway. J.J. closed the sliding side door.

Once more she navigated the roads heading home. The ride was short and sweet, which was a good thing. Though dinner time was just around the bend it was already tickling their tummies. Entering and exiting the stairwell numerous times she finally had emptied the camper's floor of the numerous bags of things she had bought. Lifting up her pet she started the locking up of the van. The Pete stood already locked up behind with the alarm system on. Sol once inside explored as he curiously inspected the buys, searching for his stuff.

Joanna repeated her night before tour of locking up. She then tackled the unpacking of the bags deposited all over the front room floor spilling into the kitchen. That task accomplished she was thoroughly famished.

The notion her pet felt the same was confirmed by his nudging his empty plate, pushing it to her feet where it stopped half on her toes.

"Gottcha ya boy, I too am hungry!" so she turned towards the cupboards she had just filled. As if a proud chef she pulled out a can of Irish stew for herself, opened it, putting it on the round to heat. Then she hauled out veggies to begin to cut them up for Sol as he watched her every move.

Though you could say Solomon was mute in a way his actions, body language, and eyes all spoke volumes that his hissing could not.

As for now it was as if he were conveying to her, "Please hurry, I'm so hungry!"

Served he ate like there was no tomorrow. Joanna buttered a few slices of bread, putting the kettle on to boil for a hot coco. Getting out her plate along with the cutlery she placed them on the table, proceeding to serve her self. The warm food answered her immediate need, but what to do about Brian now that he was out to get her? Whatever has to be done she answered herself. Besides she felt lonely, now truly in need of seeing some human friends. One thing for sure Brian was not her friend.

The Kettle began to whistle almost as if signaling a brain wave J.J. had gotten. Sol looked up disgusted with the irksome kettle. J.J.'s idea was she would throw a party to inaugurate her new apartment. No one knew to her knowledge its where about or that she had one. She could get some CD's out of the truck to play on the sound system; go buy a bottle of wine or two plus a case or two of beer. Yes a wine and pizza party. We could follow up by beer with card games. Now that would be a change, it would even be fun to dance or just listen to music with friends. Pleased with her idea she stopped the annoying kettle's whistle to the joy of the frustrated iguana. She made her coco then began to look for the numbers of a few friends. Five would be perfect, she had made up her mind. Besides she had toilet paper now for everyone she giggled to herself.

The party was on. Nelly along with Bart, a couple she knew could come that evening. Walter with his wife Ethel also accepted as well as a friend from work who also said yes. No he was not a big strapping male, but one with a sense of humor by the name of Kartoon. Kartoon would pick up the beer on the way to her place, while the two couples would each bring one bottle of wine. J.J. would order the pizza's when it was time according to their tastes. She set up a fresh dish of vegetables cut up too grab, dip and chew. The sauce was store bought naturally.

Joanna placed a few bowls of chips upon tables along with pickles and toothpicks. That should do.

Her other chores dispatched enabled her to continue with other preparations; so she went to get the CD's in the truck. Once there J.J. noticed footprints all around her truck. They had not been there after the last snowfall. Weird she thought. However, choosing to not freak out she reasoned as she reminded herself that there was a family that lived above her in this house. She did some self counseling telling herself to stop looking for boogie mans at every step. To be cautious for sure was necessary, but not to panic for nothing also. Speaking of family she decided to go warn them she was going to have a party. After all, only polite, there was going to be noise from below for a change not just above, ha ha.

Knocking on the back door she was greeted by a toddler with reddish brown hair sucking his thumb. The child eyed her though the patio doors than began to howl its head off. Must be the family's version of a doorbell J.J. laughed to herself. The young mother hurried to her son's side. A couple of minutes later she noticed Joanna at the door. Scooping up the child she opened the door motioning to J.J. to come in. Introductions were made. The young mother's name was Tess, her son's was Randy. The father was away just now gassing the car for the family trip they were embarking on. Seemingly Tess had four sisters she was proud to name; Sonya, and Melanie, were her older ones, Crystal and her little sister Elly. All the children were to be there at her mother's with their children. It was to be a big reunion, so she was all excited.

When Joanna told her about the impending party, Tess had said no problem they wouldn't even be there, plus even if they were a bit of noise every now and then was o.k.; to let it all out. The young Mom then asked J.J. to heat the furnace if she didn't mind while they were away.

Of course Joanna agreed. Taking leave she was pleased to of had met the upstairs people. Now her party could be loud with no problems, she went back to her little corner of that house feeling good.

Sol was waiting for her return; the cell was not on the table as before, but now dead silent on the floor. J.J. picked it up. Seeing Brian's number she said with determination, "not tonight Brian! I'm busy!" as she turned it off before setting it back on the table.

Then remembering she had yet to order the pizzas she turned it back on to ask her friends preferences. Her orders were put in for a six p.m. delivery before she turned off the cell again.

Getting out bowls she began to set out pretzels she remembered she had bought to add to the rest of the finger food collection. She then got out Sol's pellets to make him a dish. Chopping up a few sprigs of parsley, a bit of pepper, some radish, along with fruit she mixed in with the pellets. J.J. put the drops in his water setting it down with the food for when her pet would want them.

After cleaning up her mess she was now almost ready, even looking forward to the evening. She set up the sound system, getting out a few packs of cards, in addition to a pad with pens. It should be a fun evening. She set the table for six sitting down to survey her preparations. It would do she decided, then got up to get ready by showering and changing. Sol of course accompanied her in the rain room, later begging to be dressed to in his new vest he saw on the bed.

At last both were ready along with the wee apartment.

Half an hour later her guests arrived with the drinks. J.J. along with Sol greeted them genuinely pleased to see them. Sol got the attention he wanted so he was delighted. Joanna served wine for the first toast to the apartment, just as the pizza man arrived with all their goodies. They sat eating while trading tales with soft music in the background. All together it was an enjoyable well animated meal. That is, all except for Sol, who now bored with the human activities went to watch out the window. He figured he could lend Mistress to these people with no problem.

Bart and Nelly told tales of their two children that had them chuckling. These proud parents were wrapped around the little fingers of their kids, and they knew it too. J.J told of Big Al along with the parrot Regan, which had her guests laughing. She went on to tell them of how she had been put out of two hundred and fifty bucks at work which had them cracked up giggling.

Just then Kartoon said, "Hey J.J. why don't you tell us of the guy who came looking for you at work, he tried to get Rick to give him your address, but Rick held firm saying it was not company policies."

"What guy?" J.J. asked truly intrigued now.

"The muscle bound impolite guy who tried to rattle Rick's cage this week. Rick didn't take it, he had him escorted out by The Man with a little help from Bouncer!" he reported. "The guy was really a jerk plus he sure could cuss like it was nobodies business. He was loud mouthed till Bouncer got fed up and clouted him." He continued the tale, "Bouncer banged him on the top of the head, oh yes he did, the guy buckled like a sac of rotten potatoes. So we set him in his car, a blue sports car leaving him to stew. It was the day you arrived from your last trip to be exact. It all happened about half an hour before you arrived. Didn't you see him, he was still in his car when you got in? He must of come to his senses for he left not long after you did!"

"Shoot no, I didn't see him, why didn't you say something?" she inquired putting two and two together.

"Well Rick told us to shut up, that you seemed washed up or not well, that he'd fill you in the next time around." Kartoon explained.

"Gee thanks Kartoon, I would have preferred knowing. The jerk is my brother in law who is freaking out looking for his wife, Sara, you met Sara?" she prompted.

"Yes," they confirmed in unison before J.J. continued.

"Well this jackass beat her up, now he wants her back, which is impossible due to the circumstances. Sara is in hiding where only I know where. Only we know the true story or most of the story, besides the sawed off piece of cow plop who hurt her. Brian is laying bricks wondering how it will all turn out, now of late he is getting very nasty towards one and all. He even went so far as to threaten me in the mall today, but Sol whipped him good making him back off!"

Looking forward to changing the subject she went on to tell of her time with the manager of the mall. They all found it hilarious laughing till their sides hurt.

Beer and wine flowed freely that evening; food was guzzled just as freely. Many card games were played to the tunes of C.C.R., AC/DC, plus some favorite retro music blaring loud as she could get it. They even danced or tried to because in the end they were a bit tipsy. Around two a.m. her guests left in their taxies leaving J.J. alone with Sol. Once again she said "To hell with it, in the morning!" to the chaos left behind falling into bed.

Solomon did not sleep cuddled to Mistress's face that night. She stank to high heaven of the stuff she had drunk. He felt woozy just breathing it! Humans, poisoning themselves! He would just have to do the first watch he figured for she was out like a light; still wearing her clothes as he his vest. The small apartment was still well illuminated, but the last song had just played allowing the system to shut off. Placing himself at her feet he hunkered down glad the men had lit the furnace before leaving, they had even stoked it up for the night. The heat was glorious.

Brian had from afar watched Joanna's place. Once the guests had at last left, he came a bit closer. However, he warily stayed out of the light pouring out of the windows or at the door. By the Pete, careful not to touch the thing or set off the alarm he watched with much interest. So much interest he did not know he was being watched also by other eyes hid in the dark alley.

Brian felt cold, miserable, very fed up of all the waiting along with spying. He wanted action! To boot, with all this hogwash he'd caught a damn cold, his nose was stuffed. Sinus troubles played havoc with his breathing as well as thinking. He felt awful, with watery eyes in this freezing weather which was not helped by the massif headache left over from that bull that had clouted him. All in all, everything was slowing down his thinking process that wasn't very fast in the first place. He blamed Sara for all his troubles, then Joanna for all his health problems.

He fantasized about how he would make them both pay dearly for going against his will. They were not the first to of stood in his way or been lined up for removal.

He barely felt his toes or finger tips now. An hour had passed since they had left, he fussed sniffling while stifling a cough, "What the f . . . hell is she doing still up?" he wondered angrily in a low voice.

The other watcher surveyed Brian's discomfort pleased he suffered so.

Hearing his comment low as it was the silent person had a feeling that the snake would strike soon. Be it from fear, total boredom, or just for the pleasure. They waited.

In her fuzzy dreams Joanna out of blue eyes surveyed two dark shadows, who in turn surveyed . . . , "now was that her Pete? What was her Pete doing in her dream this time?" her muddled mind tried to straighten itself out. Sluggish, none too sober from the combination of booze as well as accumulated sleep deprivation, she tried to dream as she tried to sleep. "The sun seems to be shining!" for her lids rebelled against the light as she dozed on muttering in her sleep, befuddled and foggy.

Sol listened; feeling uneasy, for Mistress had never been in this state before. He felt uneasy for a lot of reasons lately, nor were they all due to his call of the wild or desire to have a green mate. It sure had been active lately, even tonight. But she seemed to enjoy herself then at least he deducted, satisfied he fell into a light sleep himself.

Impatient, Brian edged closer to the house. He worked at staying out of the pools of light from the half drawn blinds. He braved it to the door, where he eagerly tested the knob. It turned without restraint egging him on to enter the stairwell. In a way he felt safer under the cover of the entrance. In another sense he was now quite excited. His heart rate was pounding quickly now as he cautiously went slowly down the stairs. A bit giddy from his bad cold plus all the excitement he leaned against the wall as he descended; glad to be out of the wind at least.

At the foot of the stairs he peered into the chaotic well lit room.

It was littered with bottles, cans in addition to left over food. What a slob, he thought to himself. It must have been one hell of a party. He wondered if Sara was here or still at the bottom of the lake?

Turning to once again verify his back he did not see an iguana slip from the room. Sol aimed to climb the high torch lamp by the door, which was one of the rare lights not on. Sol sat in the top light dish waiting to see who would enter. He had a bad feeling about that person in black!

Brian returned to peek through the door window. Braver, now reassured, he slowly raised his hand taking the knob in it. It also turned without resistance.

"Stupid woman!" he hissed low but out loud. This of course alerted the awaiting iguana. It confirmed in his language that this was definitely an enemy to hiss like that. Solomon prepared himself for another super spring if need be.

Brian inched open the door, waited a moment than stepped in.

He closed his eyes just for an instant letting the glorious heat envelope him. That was the moment Sol sprung from his perch landing on his head. Sol's hind legs with their deadly claws hung down his face though he had managed a powerful spring. Righting himself the reptile scratched deep, drawing blood as he cut into frozen flesh.

Brian screamed in pain. Sol scratched even more while holding onto the woolen cap whipping with his tail the hands that were trying to grab him.

Joanna hearing the scream still dressed to the point of wearing her cowboy boots entered upon the scene. Going to aid her pet she started kicking his shins fiercely while wind milling punches all over. Out numbered and blinded by his own blood, Brian tripped over a wine bottle. He spun falling to the ground amongst cans and litter gasping. Blood now all over his coat, besides on the floor, he went for the gun's butt that showed from his pocket.

J.J. grabbed Sol aiming for the door. She slammed the door shut behind her just before a blast from the gun thundered. J.J was presently blinded also, but by fear. So much that she did not see the man coming on the run to her rescue. Not knowing what to do, having neither her keys with her, nor her cell phone; not counting she was more than a little drunk still, she ran off into the night trying to gain some time to think. The aim was to survive, yet she was ready to battle. Just right there now it was to figure out how and where. Joanna hoped this was the last of it! Meaning the final battle; where he would spill the beans, making her witness to his confession. The trick was to survive it all, yet she didn't have her gun, or any other hand weapon. She reasoned while still on the run that she must hide, or find help for now.

Chapter 22

ON THE BRIDGE

ONCE OUT ON the street Joanna headed for the over pass bridging her side with the other over the auto route. She shoved Sol while on the run into the bulky sweater she still wore over her t-shirt. She kept going with all she could muster. Solomon hung on like the lizard he was. At four a.m. in the morning there was no one about.

Unknown to Joanna another man had been on the run to see what Brian was up to; especially after he had mistaken the high-pitched scream for being that of a woman's. He had run from the Pete's shadow just in time to hear the gun shot. Worried he had lunged towards the stairwell, but hearing the running steps he had waited to see who was coming out. Seeing the long braid whip the air as the tail of her reptile did the same, he breathed easier knowing one twin was safe at least. But before he could say a word she was off and running. Just as he was to go after her he heard cursing along with more running steps.

Waiting to see who turned up this time he backed to the wall.

A bloody man emerged; spotting the girl he sprang after her while the second man leaped for him football tackle style. Both were on the ground struggling to get the upper hand. Brian, heel that he was, used the butt of his gun upon the second man; putting him out of business for a few minutes. Seeing Joanna had too much of a head start he made for the blue sports car.

Joanna felt a sudden burst of fresh hate take over her, giving new wings to her feet as she pounded the pavement. She silently prayed, frantically hoping to achieve as much distance as possible between her and Brian. J.J. felt rather than heard Brian get into his car, now she knew without a doubt he was on her trail. She also knew it wasn't to offer her a friendly ride anywhere she would like to go. It was a one way ticket he intended for her. The ride he had in mind was according to his version of fun and vengeance on the road to Hell. In her opinion she wasn't ready to go to Heaven yet.

Still on the run her Dad's words of wisdom came to her muddled mind. Those words pertaining to our choices in life; and once again she made a clear choice. She jumped to the side over the low railing of the bridge. Just as her feet lifted off the ground the car smacked into the railing where she had last stood. Joanna was now hanging from the crossover bridge dangling over the auto route. Sol agile as well as a deft climber was not perturbed by the height nor their position, but Joanna was. He was now upon her shoulder, then climbed up her arm. There from the still vibrating side railing he tried to encourage her to swing up. This was one worried iguana for his Mistress's well being.

Brian shaken, covered in blood, got out of the crumpled car. As if an avenging bull he charged cursing. However, seeing Sol made him hesitate a moment, his mind frozen in time as he thought things out a wee bit. Sol, he turned towards the oncoming man ready to protect his beloved once again. Though Solomon now shivered in the cold his heart was full of warm love, and hot hate. Tail up, ready to strike, legs taut, ready to spring, mouth open, ready to bite; he waited once again for the perfect moment. He prepared, aiming for this moving target. His Mistress struggled. She let out little yelps of fear or pain while desperately trying to get a grip with her legs or feet to hold on better with. Her now tiring arms and hands felt heavy. They were chilled by the winds which played mercilessly over her aching body. Time for both Sol, and J.J seemed to be in slow motion as Brian came ever closer now to do his worse.

Seeing the little green monster ready to attack him once more set warning bells off in his bloodied head. He hesitated, slowing just for a few steps before the railing. There he came to an abrupt stop. He admired his pray as she dangled tantalizingly from the side. Rage engulfed him.

The allure of merrily giving a few bangs with his strong fists to make her let go enthralled him. He wanted her to fall! Yes, to fall with any luck to her death. The desire blinded him to all that surrounded him.

Raising his fists above his head hollering he was going to kill her like he did Sara; just like he had done to her parents: he advanced a step to make good on his threat.

Joanna was horrified as the truth of what he had bellowed sunk in.

It gave her new vigor in her efforts to save her self. Once again a shot rang through the air. Its thunder surprising all three of them, for they had not been the ones to fire. Iguana, Joanna, along with Brian, all in wonder froze for an instant.

Brian swung around. He had an expression of disbelief upon his face as he clutched a newly bloodied shoulder. Self disgust enveloped him as he tottered near the railing. Brian watched the other man running towards the scene. "Why didn't I think of that?" he said in awe of his own stupidity just before he lost balance to flip accidentally over the railing.

Akin to a piece of dirty laundry he now by one hand hung dangling over the Decarrie auto route, along with J.J. His blood encrusted face sneered almost eye to eye with Joanna. Sol made busy scratching and biting the hands that sought to inflict pain or harm upon his Human.

Running feet could now be loudly heard slapping upon the pavement.

This however did not stop Solomon or even give him cause to look up.

Brian loosing his grip due to the pain inflicted by the little green monster frantically sought to grab a safe hold. Joanna's long braid caught his eye. He tried to take hold of it using his injured arm that was out of his attacker's reach for the moment.

At first, Joanna hysterically tried to get away from his touch by shaking her head screaming at him. Just then reason steeped up to bat.

It whispered in her now clearing mind; "Let him have it, let it be the kiss of death for this maniac, let him grab it!" So she forced herself to calm down, obeying her thoughts.

Brian now desperate along with riddled with pain grabbed that tantalizing rope like braid. He considered it at the moment to be his lifeline as well as the possible instrument to her demise. Sol, horrified that Brian had Mistress's hair gave one impressive whip at that precise moment upon the deeply cut bleeding hand. The sting of his mighty feat made the bloody man let go of the railing to swing towards Joanna holding the long slack braid. As Brian swung forth he lost height as he went. Unexpectedly however before his body slammed into J.J's the now taut braid's clip let go!

An impressed Brian looked in wonder at Joanna baffled saying, "Sara?" he questioned as he began to fall. Holding onto the mussed braided hank of cut hair he stared up at her all the way down.

J.J. looked down watching his decent hoping she would not be next. Into Joanna's, and Sol's view a familiar battered blue rabbit with peeling paint rolled as fast as it's little engine could go. Brian hit the top of the vehicle denting it badly, but the car did not even slow down let alone stop. He bounced off over the hatch back to fall to the pavement motionless. Joanna to her shame felt great dismay all of a sudden; she had truly hoped the racing Rabbit would run over him!

The car disappeared under the overpass as she heard a sexy Texan drawl shouting, "Hold on, I'm a coming!" The disembodied voice was quickly followed by a heart stopping head of thick blond hair. A worried green eyed giant's familiar face came to look over the edge.

Sol whipped this smiling face now at his height causing a welt to appear almost immediately. Backing off holding his face between his hands, Gregory hollered, "Tell him to back off!"

Joanna groaned, "Sol!" he's trying to save me boy, let him do it . . . I can't hold on much longer!" Joanna, slightly discouraged, weakly pleaded with the two males supposedly trying to help her! At that moment sirens could be heard cutting through the frigid city's early morning air.

Joanna looked down one more time, an ambulance accompanied by a police car had stopped by Brian's body. Sirens still wailed from other vehicles on their way to the bridge. Sol backed off long enough for Gregory to heave J.J. over the railing. The distrustful iguana sprang to Mistresses shoulder as she was finally lifted over. He would not let her be hurt again without a fight.

At last safe on solid ground the weak Joanna swayed. Sol climbed to her head as Gregory steadied her. Looking Greg almost eye to eye now, Solomon fell in love with the green set looking back at him. The war weary wee lad sensed he meant them no harm. Joanna leaned against the strong hard chest she had so often dreamed of. Sol went to the mountain of a man's shoulder, a better perch to survey the surrounding activity.

Within the warm clasp J.J.s chilled body seemed to come alive. Joanna surveyed some inquisitive on lookers who lined the sidewalk.

Quite a few had been roused from their sleep. Heck, not surprising, what with the sirens, plus the entire show time complete with flying bullets. Not to forget the screeching and yelling by both her, along with Brian as Sol did his thing. Of course with all that there was the metal crash of Brian's car when he had hoped to crush her. Some were still in nightdresses or pajamas with winter coats and boots hastily threw on. Curious they lined the street trying to know more, see or hear more.

As Joanna took all this in one dark black head in particular amidst the crowd caught her attention. Relief washed over as well as through her. She felt an overwhelming sensation of being loved. The other woman smiled then waved back at her! Was this a mirage, a dream, a vision, her angel, a daydream, real, or just hopeful thinking? Joanna wondered as she closed her eyes to refocus. Opening them again the person she sought was no longer to be seen among the curious spectators. Tears of disappointment welled in her eyes as Gregory cooed soothing words rubbing her cold body cuddled into his. He had mistakenly deducted that shock had set in.

"This has been one hell of a party!" Joanna boohooed while pushing her now throbbing head closer yet against that inviting warm body, listening to the steady throb of his heart. Sol, he had just staked a claim by crawling into the open coat seeking the warmth and comfort he needed. According to him humans wasted time before getting what or to where they wanted to be. His instinct said cold, this body was good, warm as well as available so he took what he needed doing no harm.

Mistress was a bit slower in these things. Time he figured would bridge over her innocence.

Chapter 23

LOOSE ENDS

THE AMBULANCES TOGETHER with the police sirens at last came to a sudden stop. The vehicles stood about ten feet from where the threesome huddled. Like in the movies all seemed to jump out at the same time to come towards them like a charging herd. Gregory held her till they had to separate due to the ambulance people wanting to check them over. He was taken to one ambulance while she was led to another.

Nevertheless they could see each other through the open doors.

Gregory sat on one side of the ambulance as they were checking his head cleaning the matted blood to see the cut. He had a nice bump but did not need stitches for the size of the cut. Sol who had still been with him was now on the other bunk facing him while an attendant comically checked him over. Solomon had a few broken bleeding nails.

Surprisingly the little guy let them clean, disinfect then bandage them up. He was treated as royalty for all talked about how the wee guy had been loyal as well as fearless in battle to save his Mistress.

In Joanna's ambulance they checked her legs cleaning out minor cuts making sure they were also disinfected. Her hands were the worse for ware however so they took care of them. They verified for hurts she may not know of making sure no bones were broken. Questions began to well in her throbbing head. She eyed Gregory across the way suspiciously.

"Tell me Inspector, who do you work for?" she called over because the name Connor Thorpe had came to mind thinking back to the newscast she had seen.

"An interested party," he replied, "A woman, I'm a private investigator now," he supplied filling her in, "and I've been working with the police here keeping them well informed."

"What's her name?" she called back wanting to get to the bottom of this. "What does she look like, where did you meet, how much she been paying you?" Once having drawn a breath, she matter-of-factly pinned on her last question, "and why?"

He fired back the answers, "Don't know, don't know, never, none of your business, she said she was worried a crime was to happen concerning one of the two Miller twins, stating that Brian Thorpe was a dangerous man."

Stunned by the weird answers for various reasons; she worked to figure out the system he had used to answer. Smiling now she realized he was playing one of her own word games with her.

"What do you mean you never saw or asked her name, furthermore why is it none of my business how much she paid you, plus just how did she manage to pay you without your finding out who she was? Joanna shot the ball back to his court.

"Never, it was all via phone. I asked, but she didn't answer, telling me to just call her Sadie for reference." He caught Joanna's sudden intake of breath as a reaction to that name, but continued on. "Cash money was deposited into my account over the counter in regular payments never missing a beat at various banks, never the same one twice, I tried to catch her!" he replied visibly ashamed a woman had outsmarted him.

A smile played on Joanna lips as tears welled in her eyes once again, in a softer voice she asked, "Did you try the surveillance cameras?"

"Yes, but she always wore baggy clothes; a woolen cap pulled down, a scarf with big glasses, like thousands of other people in winter, making me unable to identify her. Especially since she was depositing not stealing thus she wasn't committing a crime paying her bills. I had no grounds to pick her up even if I had cornered her. Plus she also wore gloves, no finger prints! I decided to leave her her privacy she worked so hard at keeping," he added on as justification to his incapacity of finding who the mystery woman was.

Typically male Joanna determined to find a way to boob it and still look good as she threw another question, "You still didn't tell me how much?"

"It's still not your business, is none of your business, and never will be your business!" he answered smugly.

"Are those sparring words Officer, I mean Inspector, or a challenge?" she sassed back jumping out of the ambulance with her blanket flowing behind her like a cape. She looked like a lady super hero ready to fight.

He too jumped out of his while Sol jumped onto his shoulder, "your choice missy!" meeting her half way, "Now let me tell you something I and the police should be the ones asking questions, not you!"

"Yes Sirey, we can all ask questions, all hoping to get answers! Right now I want to know if Brian is dead, you know he who tried to kill me as well as who openly admitted other murders like my parents while trying to do me in! Going to do something about that smarty? Nice swat on the cheek you got honey, can I have my iguana back?" She shouted back or should we say up at him. She took her stand brazenly with hands on her hips to suddenly change position to hold her hurting head. Sol once again worried about mistress went down to her shoulder to cuddle her in her blanket.

A police officer who had been jotting down things while listening to the two since awhile ago stepped in to take over. He filled her in telling her that no Brian wasn't dead but must be wishing he was. Almost every bone in his body was broken. They figured though he would live to face charges of attempted murder for her plus premeditated murder of her parents.

This made Joanna feel a little bit better. Wouldn't George be pleased?

"Odd thing, however, they had to pick blue paint out of cuts, off the guy's clothes too. Has anyone got an idea where that came from? The officer asked?

"Nope!" Gregory had drawled matter of factly.

J.J. well she had just opened wide her innocent blue eyes saying at that point in time she was too busy trying to hold on to make sure Brian was safe and sound. She had not lied, nor stretched the truth either really, just brought attention to what she was doing. And it worked.

Satisfied, the officer proceeded with his questions till Joanna thought her head was going to explode. Even Gregory seemed pretty well fed up and out of sorts. The officer realizing that it was enough for now left saying he would be in contact with both of them, tagging on . . . to stick around.

Brain and Sara's car was hauled away just as he was. The two empty ambulances left along with the police cars after offering the two a ride.

The crowd had dispersed. Nothing else was going on. So at last, all that was left to do was to go home.

Only J.J. holding Sol wrapped in her blanket with Gregory were left.

They stood staring at each other. At odds for both were trying to figure out what was going on inside themselves.

"What are you staring at!" she asked, "just as what are you doing still here?" her discomfort along with her bad humor began showing.

"Number one, at a female banty rooster clocked in a blanket freezing, probably hurting like hell, and in a bad mood too. Problem is, hard to believe but true, she's still cute though comical. Number two, at an iguana who if he freezes will look like a long green lollipop. Number three, my car is in the alley behind your place." Then last but not least, he said to stick around; "so want to go for breakfast so I can finish asking questions while maybe giving a few answers also? Food and coffee are good for a hangover sometimes." Gregory answered unsuccessfully stifling a laugh.

"Yea so they say! This is a first for me Inspector Gadget. I usually know when to stop. Right now all I want is some Tylenol. I feel stiff all over plus the head ache. You can follow me home for breakfast, but you get to cook while I pick up the mess. The Cop said they had taken their pictures so I could go home now." So she did she as she started to walk towards her home leaving him there to figure out what he was going to do.

He followed like a well trained puppy watching the blanket move as her hips did their thing, "Which twin are you he called out?" still unsure of it all, "and where is the other?

"Why we are identical, so a bit of both I guess, but you can call me J.J., as for the rest; not of your business, none of your business, and never will be!" she flung over her shoulder at him.

"Are those sparring words, or a challenge?" he whipped back.

"Both, are you up to it?" she chuckled.

"Don't know, but I'm hungry and willing to test it out!" Gregory replied unsure as to what he was getting himself into with this odd little bag of wonders.

"Good! Now shut up till I get some Tylenol will you?"

Obeying he did so, while following her in silence all the way home like a lost sheep. Joanna wondered during the walk if the way to a man's heart really was through cooking and food? If so she had a feeling he wouldn't be satisfied with just cut veggies or fruit like the other male in her life. So she guessed . . . she was in trouble again! Maybe restaurant food would bridge the gap?

Chapter 24

INTO THE NEXT

JOANNA ROLLED OUT of bed in the darkened room. She felt a lot better after her much needed snooze. Though she still suffered stiffness along with cuts n scrapes who all at this moment seemed to say: "I am here."

Feeling rested J.J was glad the hang over was gone. Immediately after turning she froze, to drink in the sight. It sure was easy on the eye looking at the beautiful sleeping man sitting in a chair by her bed. He as if a proud father held Sol also asleep cradled in his big arms.

"Traitor!" she thought as she eyed her loyal pet through this whole part of the episode now dozing where she wished she could be. She tip toed out of the room picking up her cell on the way to the bathroom. Roles were now reversed;

Joanna, was the one green with envy!

Sitting on the throne with the door three quarters closed J.J. turned on the cell. She called George hoping she would be telling him the news before the newscast. Turned out she was late, plus the elderly couple had been out of their minds with worry trying to get hold of the twins.

Joanna filled them in leaving out the fact she had been drunk as a loon when it had all blew up. Clara went for a coffee. Joanna then told George how almost every bone in Brian's body was broken, stating that his wish in a way had come true. Clara back on line J.J reassured them apart from a few cuts along with some bruises she was physically o.k.

Sitting on the bowl Joanna came to the hard part. It was the talking about her parent's death. She told them how Brian had confessed to her his having been the author of their demise. J.J. went on to say he had seemingly doctored their car brakes with intention of killing them, as he was trying to kill her as well as Sara. She also spoke of how one police officer had said Brian's out rage was equal to his pain as he screamed out his hate. He had howled his deception when told she was still alive.

The Tisson's were scandalized! They said the newscast had just said there had been an admission to another murder by the offender. This of course had them worried as to whom they were talking about. Clara and George had feared in the very bottom of their hearts that it was Sara they were talking about. The news caster had said to their relief that a lady trucker had survived the attempt on her life.

They cried together on the phone. Out poured tears of relief coupled with fear, tears of pain yet some of joy, tears of regret yet of hope and thankfulness. Another hand had just been dealt them and they had to make do doing their best with what they had! Clara hung up going to get more coffee to cry over. George stayed on the line waiting to hear what he felt Joanna was holding back.

Joanna gulped back tears, trying to overcome the hurt. She took a deep breath to say, "I don't know if it was an answer to a prayer, a mirage, a miracle, an angel or the real thing? But I saw Sara in the crowd afterwards, and she was smiling at me as she waved!" To the silence she added, "and it felt so good to see her, wherever she is, she knows, plus she's o.k., she seems happy now!"

A new boohoo session started as they once again cried together, getting comfort in the shared mixed feelings. Clara got back on the other phone just as they finished their conversation drying up the waterworks.

After all J.J. had been through, the Tisson's were worried about her being alone; so they invited her home to rest up. Joanna had shyly admitted that at the moment she was not alone. Like a school girl she confessed that the Inspector Gregory Armstrong was looking after her for the moment. She did not tell them he was asleep in her bedroom . . . even though he was on a chair rather then in her bed. She promised to visit as soon possible asking timidly if she could bring a friend along?

Of course the elderly couple was curious, but knew their J.J. enough to not ask unwanted questions. When the time came she would spill the beans and not before! They were however intrigued as to who the friend may be, deducing that the Mr. Armstrong may be the one. Just as they were curious to how much a friend he was. However the two old wise owls had a vague idea that the Inspector could well be the good person needed indeed.

They reassured her that there was no problem at all. At the same time they confirmed that it would be a pleasure to have her with or without company. Then they asked if it was the girls again, Didi and Leni? J.J. said that it wasn't them they were off abroad. The elderly folk smiled at each other then said all she had to do was land in or call ahead if they wanted some fancy cooking.

Joanna promised she would call for that delicious fancy cooking if and when. She said goodbye after expressing how much she loved them before hanging up.

Getting up, she pulled the chain. Joanna undressed to get into the shower. There she discovered just how many bruises she now sported to accompany her painfully stiff muscles. Just then another thought made her smile. She was pleased that Brian must be feeling even worse, much

much worse. Joanna thanked God she and Sol had made it through with much better fair. She continued to shower contented as well as secure in that knowledge.

Sol hearing the rain room working went to join Mistress crawling out of his warm human hammock. He too felt a few aches along with pains a spell in the warm rain would help. As most always after scratching at the tub he was lifted in.

Another male began to scratch at the door. Through the ajar door he was looking towards the closed shower curtains which allowed just a vague but tantalizing form to be seen. He drew breath to be heard above the running water.

"Can I get in too?" he asked, genuinely wanting to, obviously for more than one reason. Such as he was now hurting in more ways than one.

"No!" J.J. shouted over the rush of the water, "You can use it afterwards, with or without Sol."

"Ok, but when we go to Frampton, can we go in your truck? I've never rode in one of them!" He pleaded wanting to at least get something he wanted!

"You were listening!" she accused "It's my job to inspect and detect plus use any potential way without harming if possible to find out things" he purred back, "You sure you really don't want me to inspect you there now to detect how bad you are hurt?"

"No, but be nice, be patient, maybe one day you will get to kiss the booboo's!" she purred back teasing yet serious, "For now, why don't you get us something to eat?"

"Why do I get to do all the cooking?" he whined leaving to do so.

"Believe me it is in your best interest!" she answered, "So find us something to eat, since I can't seem to get rid of you!" she tacked on shutting off the shower wondering where all this was going to lead too.

There was still a lot to be said, or yet to be known, while a lot still hid, as well as to be found out. His being a man of the law did complicate life a bit, yet it did save her. Sara where and what are you now . . . Alive or dead? I need to know! At times I think I am going crazy. Maybe I have split personalities now? O Lord I hope all these loose ends finish tied with a bow, instead of a bunch of ugly knots.

For now I shall concentrate on Sol and Greg. Mmmmmm breakfast smells real good. It also had an interesting side dish that just offered itself. Yet for now she'd better do the dishes and cleaning before temptation had her walking down another road today and for awhile yet.

Yep, she felt she was in trouble again, but what kind of trouble she really didn't know . . . yet.

ABOUT THE AUTHOR

THIS BOOK BLOOMED while on the road realizing this author's dream of being a long distance trucker while teamed with her second husband.

She says: I traveled thirty-six States, Ontario, plus Quebec. I even took the class one drivers course completing my dream and vision while totally falling in love with the truckers way of life. Here I invite you to experience the invisible bond of twins as one twin vigilante alongside her comically possessive iguana weaves a mystery while framing a murderer. All packaged with discovering more worries while trucking through Canada/U.S.A. Follow their quest through a saga of three projected books by me, Tikat.

Tikat, is my handle name in trucking as well as too many friends. I am still living in Quebec, Canada. I am a 1958 model, born and raised in the country being the eldest child as well as the only daughter in a family with two brothers.

I was, guess in reality still am, as always a tomboy who knows when to be a lady. I'm a mother of five wonderful daughters from her first disastrous marriage, now a grandmother well blessed with eight grandchildren. Today, I am a wife to my beloved second husband, as well as a stepmother to a darling son. My husband, who is a trucker of over near forty years experience, shared with me his love for trucking on and off the road. We are both now retired from long-distance driving but hold many warm memories.

To my credit I have published poetry, as well as have won some awards, along with having exposed artworks at a museum on several occasions as well as crafts, and crocheting at fairs. I also have two books published called "Food for Thought" book one and book two, Christian based books. I have had the pleasure to do an interview for a worldwide radio station speaking on Autism and poetry for an hour with Erik Estabrook. I have won the title of Global Poet of the year with Poetry with Passion. This winning blessed me with a free book publication. I still do voluntary work for the elderly at the old folk's home in my village from my home. I do crafting projects and gifts with help from someone dear, and ever so helpful, Marie Ange.

All my life I have been an active person, except for when sickness hit too hard. Now due to being slowed down by an illness, I have more time theoretically to do things I enjoy such as: writing, poetry, drawing, sculpting, painting, flower arrangements, crafting, scrap booking, self-learning, and studing, theology—in addition to woodworking. I also enjoy cooking. Just as I take pleasure in crocheting, and films in those in those stand still moments. Of course above all is my family and friends. A dream? The book becomes a film.

I am a versatile individual, having a strong faith which is still my Rock and refuge. I have touched as well as exercised many categories of work fields; from childcare, teaching to theology and more; with trucking as well as company administration and running a business in between. I am a people person who enjoys sharing thoughts and ideas. I enjoy researching subjects. Furthermore, I am self-taught in many fields. A curious person who enjoys learning, yet who finds each day is joyfully so full that often it is hard to accomplish all that needs doing. I bet many of you are saying to themselves, "tell me about it!" To which I totally agree.

This book is the result of my motto: "Every storm cloud can have a silver lining. Never give in or up. Just keep trying, while growing with the old incorporating the new." I live from the heart, ruled by the choices made by conviction—strong, not hard; soft, not weak; independent, yet loving.

J.J, or Joanna if you prefer, is a growing character; sharing, feeling, experiencing, learning; dealing with things not as she'd hoped for, but she copes.

She is prone to emotions as well as strong family and friendship ties with those who open their hearts. Loves animals as well as has a quick sense of humor to go along with mind. Yep the whiplash flash temper and answering machine for most situations has been known to surface. Of course she has faith and stumbles, falling flat, but gets up again to tally ho forward we go.

If you are wondering if she does remind me of someone, I would have to say yes . . . myself in many ways Lordy . . .

Therefore, be it known, I say a woman can walk the road of males while still being a woman inside and out if she has it in her. Just as so be it for men. May we all do what we do best, and taste while learning from the rest.

Thank you for reading and be welcome to enjoy the next installment of the story when it comes out . . . put, put . . . Tikat, for now over and out:

Tikat

P.S. Dear Readers: Please do not be offended by some strong, or loud language for this book is based upon a real industry, possible true life situations and what real people can do or can be. Also Elaine Young Vachon says it was her first ride as editor, so hold on it may be a rough ride. Do hold on, forgive n forget . . . she hopes you love her anyway. God bless you and yours. Thank you for being you and reading :) xxx